THE SUMMER FAIR TRAP

THE MILLBROOK FALLS ROMANCES

LUCY HENRY

Ebook ISBN: 978-1-997949-06-0
Paperback ISBN: 978-1-997949-07-7

Cover created by Getcovers

FREE BOOK

Use the QR code below to claim your copy of The Matchmaking Pact and find out where the old ladies of Millbrook Falls got their passion for creating couples.

CHAPTER 1

Sloane Hartwell's eight-year career ended with a cardboard box and a security escort.

As rain pelted Boston's sidewalks, she clutched her MBA certificate and wondered how "restructuring" had become corporate-speak for "your life just imploded."

Three weeks later, she was still waiting to restart her career.

Her phone buzzed. Another rejection email, this one from a consulting firm she'd worked with during her MBA program. *While your credentials are impressive, we're looking for candidates with more recent strategic experience.*

Translation: You've been unemployed too long. You're damaged goods.

Sloane opened her laptop to her bank account. $4,247.52 remaining from eight years of corporate salary. She'd sold her designer wardrobe on consignment, canceled her gym membership, stopped buying the organic groceries that used to stock her refrigerator. Her mother's voice echoed in her head: *Never become financially dependent on anyone, Sloane. That's how women lose themselves.*

Her mother had learned that lesson the hard way—choosing love over career, following Sloane's father through three failed business ventures before he left, anyway. Sloane had been twelve when they'd moved into her grandmother's basement, listening to her mother cry about wasted potential and romantic delusions.

But after all of that, here she was losing everything without even a husband to blame.

The phone rang. Aunt Bea's number.

"Darling, I've had a bit of an accident. Minor leg fracture. Could you visit?"

Twenty minutes later, Sloane had researched fracture recovery timelines, created a preliminary care plan spreadsheet, and convinced herself that Vermont was a strategic career move. She could conduct her job search remotely while providing support to her aunt—well, great-aunt, but who cares. This was a defensible gap in her resume that demonstrated family values and crisis management capabilities. She'd be back in Boston within four weeks. Six at most.

"Recalculating. Turn right in fifty feet. Recalculating. Make a U-turn when possible."

"Pick a lane," Sloane snapped at the GPS, gripping the steering wheel as Vermont's mountain roads twisted through an endless parade of trees. Trees everywhere, no billboards, and a suspicious absence of cell towers. How did people conduct business without reliable connectivity?

Her phone sat silent in the console. No emails, no LinkedIn notifications, no calendar alerts. The absence felt like a betrayal.

When Millbrook Falls appeared below, it looked like someone had designed a town specifically to violate every principle of modern urban planning. A waterfall crashed practically through the center of downtown—or what would have been the center if the waterfall wasn't there. Who builds around something like that? Streets curved instead of forming rational grids. Charming. Inefficient. Probably a nightmare for emergency services.

Her white BMW stood out among the pickup trucks and sensible sedans like a declaration of temporary status.

Aunt Bea's cottage defied every rule of resale value. Riots of blooms spilled from window boxes. Each porch step was painted a different color. Wind chimes clacked and rang in the breeze. The very example of why HOAs existed. How would anyone ever sell this place?

The front door opened before Sloane could knock. Beatrice Kinsley balanced on crutches, her leg encased in a small tower of plastic and mesh, looking as if she'd just stepped offstage from a regional theater production.

"Sloane, darling! You're here!"

"Aunt Bea." Sloane hugged her carefully, catching hints of jasmine perfume and what might be cannabis. "Your text said *minor* fracture. That cast looks serious."

"Doctors always expect the worst." Bea waved a hand, nearly toppling. "Multiple breaks, they said. Eight to twelve weeks. But I heal fast."

Eight to twelve weeks.

Sloane's stomach dropped. Her savings wouldn't last that long. Not while maintaining her car insurance, her professional association memberships, her LinkedIn Premium subscription. At least she'd already given up her apartment—there was no way she could have managed the rent while job hunting, anyway.

Now she'd need to accelerate her timeline, optimize her networking strategy, and leverage this situation into demonstrable value for potential employers. All while helping her aunt recover.

No pressure.

Inside, the cottage was an explosion of theatrical memorabilia that violated every principle of minimalist design. Playbills wallpapered the living room. Signed photographs covered the walls. Costume jewelry sparkled from every horizontal surface. It was authentic and charming and completely non-scalable as a lifestyle model.

"The physical therapist starts tomorrow morning," Bea said, settling onto a velvet sofa with a satisfied sigh. "Lovely young man. Very enthusiastic about holistic healing."

Sloane's chest tightened. Holistic healing. Great. Her therapist was probably one of those people who thought crystals cured broken bones. "I'm here to help with your recovery, not socialize. I should probably meet with your physical therapist—review the treatment plan, understand the timeline, make sure we're working from evidence-based protocols."

Bea's eyes sparkled with something that looked dangerously like mischief. "Oh darling, you're going to love Wesley."

THE DOORBELL RANG at nine AM sharp.

Sloane approved of punctuality, even if nothing else about her situation warranted approval.

She opened the door and forgot her prepared list of clinical questions.

The man on Bea's porch looked like he'd stepped out of an outdoor recreation catalog—six feet of lean muscle in scrubs the color of summer sky, dark hair curling damply at his temples, and brown eyes that radiated warmth she hadn't felt in months.

He was also smiling. At 9 AM. On a Monday.

Unnatural. Possibly a warning sign.

"Good morning!" His voice was warm enough to melt glaciers. "Beautiful day, isn't it?"

No one should be this cheerful before coffee, Sloane thought. *It violated several laws of nature.*

"If you say so," she said, keeping her voice neutral. "I'm Sloane Hartwell, Bea's niece."

"Wesley Nakamura!" He extended his hand with genuine enthusiasm. "I'm so excited to work with your aunt. And with you, of course!"

He actually did finger guns.

Did he just... finger gun at me? Who does that in real life?

When she took his hand, heat shot up her arm—his fingers calloused and warm and confident. Their eyes met for a beat too long, and she watched his pupils dilate before he released her grip.

Great. The woo-woo PT was attractive. Just what she needed.

"Get it together," she told herself firmly. *You're here to help Bea, not judge her physical therapist for being aggressively optimistic. Though men like him—warm, cheerful, probably rescuing baby birds on weekends—never looked twice at cynical corporate refugees who measured life in spreadsheets.*

"Before we begin," Sloane said, stepping aside to let him enter, "let me guess—you're going to tell me healing is a journey and we're all flowers blooming in our own unique timeline?"

Wesley's grin widened, completely undeterred by her sarcasm. "Actually, I was going to say healing is like sourdough starter—needs time, the right environment, and patience. But I like your version too! Very poetic."

He made terrible metaphors with genuine enthusiasm. This was going to be a very long six weeks.

"Sourdough," Sloane repeated flatly.

"Yep! I actually make my own. The key is consistent

feeding and not getting discouraged when it doesn't rise right away. Same with physical therapy!" He was already moving toward where Bea sat, his entire demeanor radiating helpful energy.

Sloane followed, watching him kneel beside her aunt with practiced ease. He was humming. Actually humming some cheerful tune while checking Bea's range of motion.

Like this was a Disney movie.

"So, Bea tells me you're a consultant?" Wesley said, glancing up at Sloane while gently rotating Bea's ankle. "That must be fascinating work."

"Was," Sloane corrected. "I was a consultant. Currently I'm... between opportunities."

"Ah." His expression shifted to something that looked like genuine sympathy. "That's rough. The corporate world can be brutal."

She bristled at the pity. "It's temporary. I'm actively interviewing."

"Of course!" He went back to cheerful immediately. "And in the meantime, you get to hang out in beautiful Vermont. Silver lining!"

There was no silver lining. There was unemployment, dwindling savings, and a career gap that grew more damning by the day. But Wesley was already chatting with Bea about her garden, asking about her tomato plants with the same enthusiasm most people reserved for Olympic achievements.

Sloane pulled out her tablet and began taking notes. Treatment protocols, exercise schedules, measurable outcomes. If she had to be here, she'd at least make sure Bea received evidence-based care.

"Looks like your aunt's recovery is really... gaining ground!" Wesley said, finishing his assessment. He looked pleased with himself.

Sloane stared at him. "Was that a pun? Did you just make a physical therapy pun?"

"I did!" His grin was unrepentant. "I've got a million of them. Want to hear another?"

"I absolutely do not."

"You smiled. Just a little. I saw it."

"That was a grimace of pain."

"I'm counting it as a smile. Day one: success!" He pulled out his phone and actually made a note. "Wesley's Smile Campaign, Day One—one grimace that might have been a smile."

From the sofa, Bea watched them both with undisguised delight. "Oh, you two are going to be such fun to watch."

FOR THE NEXT FORTY-FIVE MINUTES, Sloane observed Wesley work with Bea.

Despite her skepticism, she had to admit he was good at his job. Gentle but firm, pushing Bea through exercises that clearly hurt while keeping her laughing with terrible stories about his other patients. He asked about Bea's Broadway days, listened with genuine interest, and somehow made annoying physical therapy look less like medical treatment and more like catching up with an old friend.

It was... effective. Bea was doing exercises she probably would have resisted from anyone else.

Which was annoying, because Sloane wanted to find fault with his methods. Instead, she was taking notes on his approach. The way he anticipated Bea's pain responses. How he adjusted resistance based on subtle cues. His encyclopedic knowledge of adaptive equipment.

And the humming. He hummed constantly, cheerful little tunes that shouldn't have been endearing but somehow didn't grate the way she expected.

"How does your ankle feel?" Wesley asked as he helped Bea lower her leg.

"Much better, darling. You have healing hands."

"You're doing the hard work. I'm just here to guide." He packed up his equipment with efficient movements. "Same time tomorrow?"

"Wonderful," Bea said. "Sloane will want to observe again, I'm sure."

Wesley's eyes found hers, warm and knowing. "I'd be happy to have her. Always good to have a second set of eyes. Especially very organized, slightly skeptical eyes."

"I'm not skeptical," Sloane said automatically.

"You've been making notes on a tablet for forty-five minutes."

"That's called being thorough."

"It's called being skeptical." But he was smiling. "Which is fine! I like a challenge."

As he headed for the door, he turned back. "See you tomorrow! Same time, same place, same excellent attitude!"

"Only one of us has an excellent attitude," Sloane muttered.

"I know! I'm working on you." He actually did finger guns again, then left whistling.

Sloane stared after him, then turned to Bea. "Is he always like this?"

"Relentlessly cheerful? Yes. Isn't it wonderful?"

"That's one word for it."

But she was fighting a smile, and Bea definitely noticed.

This was dangerous. Not just the attraction—though that was definitely a problem—but the way Wesley looked at her like she was fascinating instead of broken. Like her cynicism was amusing rather than off-putting. Like maybe spending six weeks in Vermont wouldn't be the career death sentence she'd imagined.

And the humming. The terrible puns. The completely unwarranted optimism.

She was either going to strangle him or...

No. Not going there. She had a career to rebuild, savings to preserve, and a life to get back to. Wesley Nakamura and his stupid metaphors were just a temporary distraction.

Six weeks. She could survive six weeks of relentless cheerfulness.

Probably.

WESLEY SAT in his truck for a full minute after leaving Bea's cottage, grinning like an idiot.

Sloane Hartwell was beautiful in that buttoned-up professional way that made him want to muss her perfect hair and see what she looked like when she let go. Sharp intelligence in those eyes, protective love for Bea underneath the corporate armor, and a vulnerability she was working overtime to hide.

Also, she clearly thought he was an idiot.

Which was kind of adorable.

He pulled out his phone and texted Cora: *New patient's niece is here. This is going to be interesting.*

Cora's response was immediate: *Interesting how?*

Wesley typed out *Complicated. Beautiful. Thinks I'm an idiot. I'm going to make her smile if it kills me,* then deleted it and sent: *Interesting. Very grumpy. I like a challenge.*

Because he did like challenges. And Sloane Hartwell was definitely that.

She'd rolled her eyes three times during his explanation of holistic healing. That had to be some kind of record. Most people made it to at least five minutes before the eye-rolling started.

He was making progress!

Wesley started the engine but didn't drive away yet. Instead, he found himself mentally cataloging everything he'd noticed about Sloane Hartwell in their brief interaction.

The dark circles under her eyes despite careful makeup. The way her hand shook slightly when another email notification lit up her phone. The catch in her voice when she'd mentioned being "between opportunities." The fierce protectiveness in her expression when she'd asked about Bea's treatment plan.

She was scared. Trying to control the uncontrollable by color-coding and spreadsheets, and aggressive questioning.

She needed someone to make her laugh.

Challenge accepted.

He'd sworn off falling for women who saw Millbrook Falls as a rest stop between their real lives. Devon had been exactly that—six months of promises about maybe building something here, then a job offer in Boston and goodbye. Wesley had learned that lesson expensively.

But something about Sloane's desperate need for control, the way she gripped her tablet like a life preserver, made him want to show her that not everything needed fixing. That sometimes the best thing you could do was take a breath, trust the process, and stop measuring your worth by impossible standards.

Also, her sarcasm was hilarious. She'd called his sourdough metaphor "ambitious" in a tone that clearly meant "terrible."

He was already looking forward to tomorrow's session. Already mentally cataloging physical therapy puns to try on her.

This recovery is really gaining traction? Too obvious.

We're making joint progress? Better.

I'm not being hipsterior, but your range of motion is improving? Okay, that one needed work.

Wesley hummed as he pulled out of Bea's driveway, already planning how to make the grumpy consultant smile. It was going to be his new project. His mission. His purpose for the next six weeks.

Cora texted again: *Don't do anything stupid.*

He grinned and replied: *Too late.*

Because this was absolutely stupid. Sloane had made it crystal clear Vermont was temporary, that she had a career to salvage, a real life waiting elsewhere. Getting attached to her would be like planting annuals and expecting perennials—beautiful while they lasted, devastating when they left.

But when she'd taken his hand at the door, he'd felt that spark of connection. Seen her pupils dilate, watched her catch her breath.

She'd felt it too.

And if there was one thing Wesley Nakamura excelled at, it was impossible challenges and relentless optimism.

Sloane Hartwell didn't stand a chance.

He was already humming the tune to "Don't Stop Believin'" when he pulled into the clinic parking lot, ready to face whatever the day brought with his usual enthusiasm.

His receptionist, Cora, took one look at his face and groaned. "Oh no. You've got that look."

"What look?"

"The 'I've found a project person' look. The last time you had that look, you adopted three feral cats and convinced yourself they'd be therapy animals."

"They're great therapy animals! Mrs. Patterson loves them."

"Mrs. Patterson is allergic to cats."

"She loves them from a safe distance." Wesley dropped his bag in his office. "And for your information, this is completely different."

"Different how?"

"This is..." He paused, trying to find the right words. "This is someone who needs to learn that not everything in life requires a spreadsheet."

Cora raised an eyebrow. "And you're going to teach her that?"

"I'm going to try."

"With your terrible puns and relentless cheerfulness?"

"Exactly!" Wesley grinned. "It's my signature move."

Cora shook her head, but she was smiling. "Well, at least this should be entertaining. How grumpy are we talking?"

"Spreadsheet-before-coffee grumpy. Corporate-armor grumpy. Eye-rolled-three-times-in-one-conversation grumpy."

"Ooh. That's pretty grumpy."

"I know!" Wesley pulled up his patient schedule for the day. "It's perfect. By the end of six weeks, I'm going to have her making puns herself."

"You're insane."

"I'm optimistic. There's a difference." He grabbed his therapy bag. "Mrs. Henderson's first, right?"

"Ten minutes." Cora handed him a file. "And Wesley? Don't get too attached. Remember what happened with—"

"I know." His smile faltered briefly. "I remember."

But as he reviewed Mrs. Henderson's case notes, his mind kept drifting back to Bea's cottage. To sharp eyes and a defensive posture and the hint of a smile, Sloane had tried to hide.

He was already mentally counting down the hours until tomorrow's session.

This was either going to be the best or worst idea he'd ever had.

Probably both.

But that was fine. Wesley Nakamura had never backed down from a challenge. And making Sloane Hartwell smile?

That was a challenge worth taking.

CHAPTER 2

The next morning, Sloane woke to the sound of birdsong.

Not her alarm. Not traffic. Not the neighbor's dog.

Birds. Chirping. At an ungodly hour.

She checked her phone: 6:47 AM. In Boston, she'd have been up for thirty minutes already, checking markets, reviewing emails, planning her day. Here, apparently, the entertainment was avian.

Her inbox held three new messages—all automated job alerts for positions she was overqualified for. Nothing from the seven companies she'd interviewed with. Nothing from her network connections who'd promised to "keep an eye out."

Nothing.

Sloane pulled on running clothes and headed outside, determined to at least maintain her fitness routine if everything else was falling apart. The morning air was cool and smelled of pine and damp earth. No exhaust fumes. No coffee carts. No ambitious professionals power-walking to early meetings.

She ran until her lungs burned, trying to outpace the anxiety clawing at her chest.

By nine AM, she'd showered, dressed in what passed for casual professional wear, and positioned herself in Bea's living room with her laptop and tablet. If Wesley Nakamura thought she was going to accept his "trust the process" nonsense without pushback, he had another think coming.

She'd spent two hours last night researching evidence-based physical therapy protocols for complex fractures. Created a comprehensive treatment plan with measurable benchmarks. Color-coded the entire thing by week, exercise type, and expected progress indicators.

If he was going to treat Bea, he'd do it properly.

The doorbell rang at exactly 9:00 AM.

Punctual. She'd give him that.

Sloane opened the door, prepared to be professional and clinical and definitely not notice how his scrubs—patterned with tiny cartoon physical therapy puns today—made his shoulders look even broader than she remembered.

"Good morning!" Wesley's smile could have powered a small city. "Wow, you look ready for business. I love the organization vibe."

He was holding coffee. Two cups from a local café.

"I brought you this." He offered one. "Bea mentioned you take it black. Figured you might need fortification for my terrible jokes today."

Sloane stared at the cup. "You brought me coffee."

"Is that weird? I can take it back—"

"No." She accepted it before she could overthink. "Thank you. That's... thoughtful."

"Don't sound so surprised. I'm occasionally thoughtful." He stepped inside, and she caught that same herbal scent from yesterday—shampoo mixed with something outdoorsy.

"Though I'll admit, I'm mostly bribing you so you'll go easy on my methods today."

"Your methods are what I wanted to discuss—"

"Oh no." Wesley's grin widened. "You made charts, didn't you?"

"Evidence-based treatment protocols—"

"Color-coded?"

"That's not relevant—"

"I bet they're beautiful. Can I see them?"

Sloane found herself fighting a smile at his genuine enthusiasm for her spreadsheets. Most people looked at her organizational systems like they were filed tax returns. Wesley looked like she'd handed him Christmas morning.

"After the session," she said firmly. "I don't want to disrupt Bea's treatment."

"Fair enough." He headed toward where Bea was already settled on the sofa, humming show tunes. "But I'm looking forward to it. There's something really attractive about a well-organized critique of my professional methods."

Was he flirting with her? Through spreadsheets?

Don't be ridiculous, Sloane told herself firmly. *He's just friendly. Aggressively, insufferably friendly.*

THE SESSION WENT SMOOTHLY until Wesley suggested Bea try a new exercise that wasn't in any of the protocols Sloane had researched.

"Wait." Sloane looked up from her notes. "That's not in the standard progression. She should be focusing on range of motion exercises, not—whatever that is."

"This is a proprioceptive exercise," Wesley explained patiently. "Helps retrain the neuromuscular system after immobility. Think of it like... reminding the body how to balance."

"But the research shows—"

"The research shows lots of things. Bodies don't always read the research." He was still smiling, but there was steel underneath now. "Trust me on this one?"

"Trust you." Sloane set down her tablet. "Based on what? Your... intuition?"

"Based on eight years of clinical experience and a doctorate that cost me six figures in student loans."

"Then you should be following evidence-based protocols—"

"I am. I'm just also adapting them to the actual human in front of me instead of the theoretical patient in a study."

They were standing now, facing each other across Bea's living room. Too close. Close enough that Sloane could see gold flecks in his brown eyes, catch the scent of his shampoo—something herbal and clean that made her want to lean closer.

Also, he was still smiling. Who smiled during an argument? Sociopaths, probably.

"Your treatment approach is very..." Sloane searched for a diplomatic word. "Organic."

"Thank you!"

"That wasn't a compliment."

"I'm choosing to take it as one. See? Positive mindset." Wesley's grin turned absolutely infuriating. "You should try it sometime."

"I don't need—"

"Perhaps," Bea interjected, "we could continue this fascinating discussion after my session? I'm getting a cramp in my leg."

They both turned to her, chagrined.

"Sorry, Bea," Wesley said immediately, moving back to his patient. But not before Sloane caught him muttering,

"Though for the record, organic is totally a compliment in physical therapy circles."

He was going to be the death of her. Death by relentless optimism.

AFTER THE SESSION ENDED, Sloane pulled up her comprehensive treatment plan on her tablet. "Can we talk about your methodology?"

"I'd love to." Wesley dropped onto the sofa beside her—close enough that their thighs almost touched. "Show me what you've got."

She turned the screen toward him, pointing to her color-coded timeline. "I've mapped out a six-week recovery protocol based on current literature on complex lower extremity fractures. Green sections indicate—"

"This is incredible," Wesley interrupted, leaning closer to study her work. "How long did this take you?"

"A few hours. It's not that complicated if you know where to look for data—"

"Sloane." He turned to face her fully, and they were suddenly very close. "This is seriously impressive. The level of detail, the research citations, the way you've organized everything by priority and dependency relationships... this is amazing work."

She blinked, surprised by the genuine admiration in his voice. "But?"

"But—" He smiled ruefully. "—it won't work exactly like this. Bea's not a data point. Some days she'll do better than expected. Some days worse. We'll need to adjust constantly based on how she actually feels, not how the timeline says she should feel."

The way he crossed his arms made his scrubs pull tight across his shoulders. The patient way he explained things despite her obvious skepticism—as if he had all the time in the world and no concept of efficiency. The warmth in his voice when he said her name, as if it was worth savoring.

It was infuriating how attractive competent optimism was.

"So you're saying my research was pointless," Sloane said flatly.

"I'm saying your research is brilliant and I want to use it as a framework. But frameworks need flexibility." Wesley tilted his head, studying her. "Can I ask you something? What are you really worried about here?"

"I'm not worried, I'm being thorough—"

"Sloane."

The gentle way he said her name made her defenses crack.

"I need her to get better," she admitted quietly. "On schedule. According to plan. Because if she doesn't, I'm stuck here. And every day I'm stuck here is another day I'm not getting my career back on track. Another day the gap in my resume grows. Another day closer to being completely unhireable."

Wesley's expression softened. "So this isn't really about Bea's treatment protocols."

"I know you're going to say it's about control." Sloane laughed bitterly. "The illusion of it, anyway. If I can make detailed enough plans, color-code enough spreadsheets, track enough variables... maybe I can prevent everything from falling apart again."

"And how's that working out?"

"Obviously terribly, since I'm arguing about physical therapy with someone who makes sourdough metaphors."

"Hey, that was a good metaphor!" But Wesley was smiling. "For what it's worth? You're not stuck here. You're choosing to be here for someone who needs you. That's not the same thing."

"Feels the same from where I'm sitting."

"Maybe you're sitting in the wrong place."

Before Sloane could respond, Wesley stood and stretched. "So here's what I'm thinking. We use your incredible research as our baseline—seriously, this is better than anything I could have put together—but we build in flexibility for adjustments. I promise to explain my clinical reasoning for any deviations. You promise to trust that I'm not just making it up as I go along. Deal?"

The dare was obvious, and Sloane's competitive nature flared alongside something more dangerous—the urge to prove herself to this man who looked at her like she was a puzzle worth solving. A puzzle who needed more whimsy in her life. His word. *Whimsy.*

"One condition," she said.

"Name it."

"I want to see what you do. Your whole practice. How you work with other patients. See if this flexible, intuitive approach actually gets results or if you're just charming people into thinking they're improving."

Wesley's grin turned wicked. "Are you saying I'm charming?"

"I'm saying you're suspicious."

"Suspicious. Right." He was definitely laughing at her now. "So you want to shadow me for a day? Watch me work with other patients?"

"Yes."

"And if my approach works—if you see real results despite my terrible lack of color-coded spreadsheets—you'll ease up on the control thing? Let Bea's recovery happen at its own pace?"

Sloane bristled. "I don't have a control thing."

"Sloane. You made a spreadsheet to organize your spreadsheets."

"That's just good information architecture."

"It's adorable chaos." Wesley held up his hands at her glare. "Sorry, adorable control tendencies. Much better. So—deal?"

She shouldn't agree to this. Should keep her professional distance, stick to her plans, avoid spending unnecessary time with someone who made her feel off-balance.

But the challenge in his eyes, the way he waited for her answer without pushing, the hint of respect underneath all that insufferable optimism...

"Fine. One day. But I'm taking notes."

"I wouldn't expect anything less." Wesley moved toward the door, then paused. "Fair warning—my practice is very community-integrated. Lots of coffee breaks and front porch conversations and asking patients about their tomato plants. It's going to offend every one of your efficiency instincts."

"I'll survive."

"Will you? Because you might have to experience things like... human connection. And inefficient small talk. And old ladies who want to show you pictures of their grandchildren." He was grinning openly now, enjoying her discomfort.

"I think I can handle old ladies and their grandchildren."

"We'll see. Tomorrow, eight AM. Wear comfortable shoes." He opened the door, then turned back. "Oh, and Sloane? That research you did last night? The amount of work you put into understanding how to help Bea? That's not control. That's love. You should probably let yourself recognize the difference."

He left before she could respond, humming as he walked to his absurdly beat-up Subaru.

WESLEY MADE it to his truck before pulling out his phone and texting Cora: *I think I just fell in love with a spreadsheet. This is a new low.*

Her response was immediate: *Please elaborate.*

Bea's niece created a comprehensive six-week PT protocol. Color-coded. Citations. Dependency mapping. It's beautiful. Also she thinks I'm a charlatan.

Sounds promising.

She's coming on rounds tomorrow to prove I'm making it all up.

Wesley.

What?

Don't do the thing.

What thing?

The thing where you fall for someone who's already planning their exit. The Devon thing. Remember Devon?

Wesley stared at his phone, jaw tight. Of course he remembered Devon. Hard to forget someone who'd promised maybe-forever and delivered six months before taking a job offer that "was too good to pass up, babe, you understand."

He understood perfectly. Millbrook Falls had been a rest stop. A charming adventure before returning to real life.

This is different, he typed.

How?

She's grumpier. And makes better spreadsheets.

That's not different. That's just Devon with organization skills.

Wesley wanted to argue, but Cora was right. Sloane had made it crystal clear that Vermont was temporary, that she had a life to get back to. She was exactly the wrong person to develop feelings for.

Except.

Watching Sloane defend her position with precision had been doing dangerous things to his self-control. She'd stood there with her color-coded charts and fierce intelligence, completely unaware that she was the most compelling woman he'd met in years.

But beneath the criticism, he'd seen what she couldn't hide—the desperation to control something, anything, in a life that had spun completely beyond her grasp. The research she'd done hadn't been about doubting his methods. It had been about protecting someone she loved while feeling utterly powerless.

He understood that. More than she probably realized.

I'm not falling for her, Wesley typed. *I'm just... intrigued. By the challenge.*

The challenge of what? Converting a corporate workaholic into someone who appreciates Vermont living? That worked great last time.

She's not Devon.

You're right. Devon never made you defensive. You're already in deeper than you think.

Wesley tossed his phone onto the passenger seat and started the engine. Fine. Maybe he was intrigued. Maybe he'd spent the entire morning hyperaware of every time Sloane bit her lower lip while concentrating. Maybe her withering look when he'd made that sourdough reference yesterday had been unexpectedly hot.

The difference was—and this was important—Devon had never looked lost underneath the confidence. Had never gripped a tablet like a shield against uncertainty. Had never needed someone to show him that worth existed outside achievement.

Also, Devon had never made him laugh by being sarcastic. Sloane's eye rolls were becoming a highlight of his day, which probably said something about his mental health.

Beautiful, grumpy, spreadsheet-wielding trouble, he thought as he drove out of Bea's driveway.

Tomorrow he'd show her his practice. The coffee breaks,

the front porch conversations, the way healing happened in the spaces between appointments. If she couldn't see the value in that, fine. At least he'd know.

But something told him Sloane Hartwell saw more than she admitted. That underneath all that corporate armor was someone who desperately wanted permission to slow down, to trust, to believe that not everything required a plan.

He was going to give her that permission.

Whether she liked it or not.

AFTER WESLEY LEFT, Sloane found Bea watching her with undisguised amusement.

"What?"

"Nothing, darling. Just admiring the sparks flying around my living room. Should I have kept a fire extinguisher handy?"

How could Bea see thing so wrong? "We were having a professional disagreement—"

"You were flirting."

"I was not—" Sloane stopped. Took a breath. "He's infuriating."

"Mmm. Infuriatingly attractive?" Bea's raised eyebrow was so over the top, Sloane wanted to laugh.

"Infuriatingly optimistic. He acts like everything can be solved with positive thinking and silly metaphors."

"And you're attracted to that," Bea said, making it a statement rather than a question.

She so didn't have time for this delusion. "I'm not attracted to anything. I'm professionally skeptical of his methods."

"Right. That's why you checked your appearance in every reflective surface after he arrived."

Sloane opened her mouth to deny it, then closed it again.

Had she? That was not good. She was supposed to be focused on getting her career back on track. But, thinking back, she couldn't deny Bea's point.

Damn it. She had.

"Aunt Bea, I can't—I'm not here for romance. I'm here to help you recover and get my career back on track. That's it."

"Of course, darling. Though I can't help noticing those two things aren't mutually exclusive."

"They are for me." Sloane sank onto the sofa beside her aunt. "I can't lose myself the way my mother did. My life isn't here. I need a city around me."

"Your mother didn't lose herself because she fell in love. She lost herself because she stopped making her own choices. There's a difference."

That's not what her mother said. "Not from where I'm sitting."

"Then maybe," Bea said gently, "you're sitting in the wrong place."

Sloane laughed despite herself. "That's the second time today someone's said that to me."

"Then perhaps you should listen." Bea settled back against her cushions. "Now, tell me more about this research you did. Wesley seemed genuinely impressed."

They spent the next hour discussing treatment protocols and recovery timelines, but Sloane's mind kept drifting to tomorrow. To an entire day shadowing Wesley Nakamura through his practice. Watching him work. Learning his methods.

Being near him for hours.

This is professional curiosity, she told herself firmly. *Research. Due diligence.*

But when she checked her phone and found herself hoping for a text from Wesley—maybe confirming tomorrow's plans, or making another terrible pun—she knew she was lying to herself.

She couldn't afford to be attracted to a small-town physical therapist who probably had a golden retriever named Sunshine and thought five-year plans were "limiting your possibilities."

But her body hadn't gotten the memo.

Traitor.

Her phone buzzed. Not Wesley. Another automated job alert for a position that required five years more experience than she had.

Eight weeks in Vermont suddenly felt both too long and not nearly long enough.

CHAPTER 3

Eight AM arrived with Wesley's cheerful knock and two more coffees.

"You're going to give me a caffeine problem," Sloane said, accepting the cup anyway.

"Better than the control problem you already have." He grinned at her glare. "Too soon?"

"Much too soon."

"Noted. I'll wait until at least nine AM before pointing out your control issues." He checked his watch.

Despite herself, Sloane smiled. "You're impossible."

"And you just smiled voluntarily. I'm counting that. Day three, smile number..." He pretended to calculate. "Seven? Eight?"

"You're not actually keeping track—"

"I have a spreadsheet." At her expression, he laughed. "Kidding. Mostly. Though I am mentally noting your progress toward becoming a functional human with emotions."

"I have emotions."

"You probably have spreadsheets about emotions. It's

different." Wesley headed toward his Subaru. "Come on, Grumpy. Time to see how the other half practices medicine."

They spent the morning visiting patients scattered across Millbrook Falls.

Sloane followed Wesley's disreputable Subaru in her pristine BMW, watching him in her rearview mirror. He was singing. Head bobbing, one hand occasionally leaving the steering wheel to conduct an invisible orchestra.

He was probably off-key. Enthusiastically off-key.

It should have been annoying.

It *was* annoying.

So why was she smiling?

Their first stop was a Victorian house painted a cheerful yellow. Wesley parked and waited for Sloane, his hand settling warm against her lower back as they walked up the path.

"This way—Mrs. Henderson's place is tricky to find. The walkway splits."

His touch sent heat radiating through her entire body. Damn him and his casual happy warmth.

Sloane stepped away. "I can follow a path."

"Can you? Because I saw you try to get on the highway going the wrong direction yesterday."

"GPS error."

"The GPS said 'turn left' and you turned right."

"I was testing its reliability."

Wesley's grin was infuriating. "Sure you were. Come on, Mrs. Henderson's expecting us."

MRS. HENDERSON WAS a bird-like woman in her eighties who insisted on serving them tea and showing Sloane forty-seven pictures of her grandchildren before allowing Wesley to start therapy.

"This is Matthew—he's at MIT studying engineering. Very smart boy. Takes after his grandfather."

"He's lovely," Sloane said automatically, watching Wesley set up resistance bands.

"And this is his sister Emma. She's pre-med at UVM. Wesley's alma mater! Did you go to UVM, dear?"

"I went to BU," Sloane said. "For my MBA."

"Oh, business!" Mrs. Henderson's tone suggested Sloane had confessed to tax evasion. "Well. That's... practical."

Wesley was trying not to laugh. Sloane could tell by the way his shoulders shook.

"Mrs. Henderson," he said, saving her, "shall we work on your shoulder mobility?"

For the next thirty minutes, Sloane watched Wesley guide Mrs. Henderson through exercises. He was gentle but firm, pushing her through movements that were clearly uncomfortable while keeping up a steady stream of conversation about her garden, her grandchildren, the church bake sale.

The gentle way he adjusted Mrs. Henderson's arm position. How he listened with full attention like she was the only person in the world. The competence of his hands as they worked through rehabilitation exercises.

It would be easier to resist him if he were terrible at his job. But no, he had to be genuinely good at this whole healing-people thing.

Inconsiderate.

"Your progress is really gaining traction!" Wesley said as Mrs. Henderson completed a difficult stretch.

The old woman laughed. "You and your puns."

Sloane muttered, "That's three today."

Wesley's head snapped toward her. "You're keeping count?"

"I'm documenting for future complaint purposes."

"Your dedication to my terrible jokes is noted and appreciated." His grin widened. "Want to hear number four?"

"Absolutely not."

"Your enthusiasm is overwhelming. I can really feel the support."

Even Mrs. Henderson laughed at that.

THEIR SECOND STOP was a farmhouse where a teenage athlete was recovering from knee surgery.

"This is Sophie," Wesley introduced. "Tore her ACL during soccer playoffs. She's determined to make varsity next year."

Sophie was fierce and frustrated, pushing through exercises with gritted teeth. Wesley matched her intensity, celebrating small victories and redirecting her frustration into determination.

"I should be further along," Sophie complained. "Coach says I'm behind schedule."

"Coach isn't a physical therapist," Wesley said firmly. "Your body heals at its own pace. Pushing too hard now means re-injury later. Trust the process."

Sloane caught the parallel immediately. *Trust the process.* The same thing he'd told her about Bea.

After the session, as they walked back to their cars, Sophie's mother pulled Wesley aside.

"Thank you," she said quietly. "She actually listens to you. Won't listen to me, won't listen to her coach, but you..." She trailed off, emotional.

Wesley's hand found her shoulder. "She's scared. Scared her body won't come back the way it was. That fear makes her push too hard. But she's doing great. I won't give her high-intensity work until she's ready. Really."

The woman nodded, blinking back tears.

In the car, Sloane found herself reassessing everything she'd assumed about Wesley's methods. The stories he told weren't time-wasting—they were building trust. The flexibility wasn't chaos—it was reading what each patient needed.

He was doing exactly what he'd claimed: treating whole people, not just injuries.

It was annoyingly effective.

WESLEY CAUGHT Sloane watching him during Sophie's session. Not with skepticism this time—with something softer. Understanding, maybe. Or at least the beginning of it.

Progress.

They stopped at the diner for lunch, and Wesley watched Sloane navigate the curious stares of locals with her corporate armor firmly in place. She looked out of place in her pressed linen blouse among the worn flannel and casual comfort, but something about her careful observation made him want to translate his world for her. Show her why these inefficient connections mattered.

"They're staring," she said quietly, studying the menu.

"You're new. And you arrived in a BMW. That's like announcing you're from another planet."

"Should I have rented a pickup truck?"

"Only if you can parallel park it. The trucks here are huge." Wesley ordered for both of them—he'd been coming here long enough to know what was actually good. "Give them time. Small towns are slow to warm up, but once you're in, you're family."

"I'm not staying long enough to be family."

The reminder stung more than it should have. "Right. Back to Boston as soon as Bea's mobile."

Sloane's phone buzzed. She glanced at it, and Wesley saw her whole body tense like she'd been struck. The mask slammed into place, but not before he caught a flash of devastation.

Another rejection, he realized.

The urge to pull her into his arms, to tell her those companies were idiots for not seeing her value, nearly overwhelmed his professional boundaries. Instead, he reached across the table and gently pushed her phone face-down.

"Whatever it says, it can wait until after lunch."

"It's just—"

"Another company that doesn't deserve you. I know." His voice came out rougher than intended. "But right now, you're having lunch with someone who thinks you're brilliant and overqualified for pretty much everything. So maybe take a break from the rejection parade?"

Sloane stared at him. "You think I'm brilliant?"

"Your spreadsheets are legendary. Of course you're brilliant." Wesley leaned back as their food arrived. "Also stubborn, controlling, and allergic to fun. But definitely brilliant."

"I'm not allergic to fun."

"When's the last time you did something just because it sounded enjoyable? Not strategic, not resume-building. Just... fun?"

Sloane opened her mouth, then closed it. "I went running this morning."

"That doesn't count. You run like you're being chased by performance reviews."

"How would you know how I run?"

"I saw you yesterday morning. From my apartment window. You looked miserable."

"I was exercising—"

"You were punishing yourself." Wesley held her gaze. "There's a difference."

The silence stretched between them, loaded with things neither was ready to say.

. . .

AFTER LUNCH, they had one more appointment. An elderly Chinese woman tending a garden beside a farmhouse.

"Mrs. Chiang!" Wesley called. "Didn't know you'd be here."

"Someone has to make sure Robert's tomatoes don't get blight." She straightened, studying Sloane with sharp eyes behind wire-rimmed glasses. "You must be the corporate woman from Boston. Heard you're here until Bea Kinsley recovers."

"Yes." Sloane was tired of being defined by her temporary status.

"Hmm." Mrs. Chiang's gaze traveled between Sloane and Wesley. "Wesley's always careful with temporary people. Learned that lesson the hard way."

"Mrs. Chiang," Wesley said quietly, warning in his voice.

"Just making an observation, dear boy." The woman returned to her pruning. "Though I notice you're already making exceptions to your keep professional distance rule. Interesting."

Sloane watched color rise in Wesley's face, saw him deliberately not look at her.

He's been hurt before, she realized. *By someone temporary. Someone like me.*

The knowledge sat heavy in her chest.

WESLEY WAS quiet as they drove to their final stop—a scenic overlook he claimed was essential for understanding Vermont.

"Is this another appreciate the moment exercise?" Sloane asked as they parked.

"Would you participate if it was?"

"Absolutely not."

"Then no. This is pure logistical planning." He led her to the viewing area where Mount Mansfield rose green and gold in afternoon light. "We're surveying potential wellness fair backup locations."

"The fair is already at the fairgrounds."

"Backup location. You love backup plans."

Despite herself, Sloane smiled. "You're ridiculous."

"I contain multitudes." Wesley leaned against the railing, looking out at the valley below. "Also, are you saying my puns aren't philosophical? Healing is a joint effort has layers."

"It really doesn't."

"See, that's where you're wrong. It's both about joints—the physical kind—and joint as in collaborative effort. Multi-layered comedy gold."

"That's not what comedy gold means."

They stood in comfortable silence, watching the light shift across the mountains. Finally, Wesley spoke, his voice losing its playful edge.

"This is why I stayed. After all those rejection letters, after giving up on elite athlete rehabilitation, I drove up here and realized I'd been chasing the wrong dream."

Sloane glanced at him. "That's very philosophical for someone who makes physical therapy puns."

"I wanted credentials and prestige and to prove I was good enough." He didn't look at her, just kept his gaze on the mountains. "But sitting here, watching the town below, I realized good enough was the wrong question. I should have been asking good for what?"

This wasn't the sunshiny physical therapist who annoyed her with flexibility and terrible jokes. This was a man who'd faced the same career devastation she was facing and chose something radical—contentment over achievement. And he wasn't naive about it. He'd made a conscious choice.

"What if you'd gotten those jobs?" Sloane asked quietly. "The prestigious ones?"

"I'd probably be miserable. Working eighty hours a week, treating athletes who see me as a stepping stone to their next contract, never really connecting with anyone." Wesley finally turned to look at her. "I'd be successful and empty."

"You make it sound like those are the only options. Success or emptiness."

"Aren't they? For people like us?" His gaze was steady. "You were successful. Were you happy?"

The question landed like a punch. Sloane looked away, back at the mountains. "I don't know. I was... busy. Focused. Moving forward."

"That's not the same as happy."

"Maybe happy isn't the point. Maybe the point is building something that lasts. Proving you can."

"To who?"

"To—" Sloane stopped. To herself? To her mother? To everyone who'd ever doubted? "I don't know anymore."

Standing there beside him, sunset painting his profile in gold, she wanted to ask if contentment was lonely. If choosing this beautiful, slow-paced life meant giving up the kind of ambition that had defined her for a decade. But that felt too vulnerable, too close to admitting she was considering alternatives to her master plan.

Her defense mechanism kicked in. "This is very Sound of Music. Are you going to burst into song?"

"Only if you promise to join in."

"Hard pass."

"Your loss. I do an excellent Climb Every Mountain." But Wesley was smiling now, the serious moment broken.

He turned to look at her fully, and the intensity in his expression stole her breath. The teasing faded into something warmer, more serious. He stepped closer, near enough that she felt the warmth radiating from his body.

For one suspended heartbeat, she thought he might kiss her.

Then he stepped back, humor returning like armor. "We should head back. Bea will worry. Also, I'm pretty sure you're allergic to scenic overlooks and I don't want to trigger an eye-roll emergency."

Sloane surprised herself by admitting, "It was... nice. The view. You won't win every date."

Wesley's grin was pure sunshine. "Too late. I'm already mentally composing a victory speech."

THE DRIVE back to Bea's was quiet, but it wasn't uncomfortable. Sloane seemed lost in thought, and Wesley let her be, his mind stuck on that moment at the overlook.

He'd almost kissed her.

Would have, if his brain hadn't kicked in with reminders about temporary people and keeping professional boundaries and not falling for someone who'd already bought her exit ticket.

Too late, Cora's voice echoed in his head. *Maybe you should have thought about that sooner.*

She was right. He was absolutely, completely in deeper than he thought.

Because standing there with Sloane, watching her mask drop as she admitted she didn't know what happiness looked like anymore, he'd seen the woman underneath all that corporate armor. Someone scared and lost and trying desperately to find solid ground in a life that had shifted beneath her feet.

Someone who maybe, possibly, could imagine a different kind of life if she'd just let herself try.

But Mrs. Chiang's words haunted him. *You're always careful with temporary people. Learned that lesson the hard way.*

Devon had started the same way. Temporary summer residency, clear end date, absolutely not staying. Then six months of maybe-we-could-make-this-work before reality reasserted itself in the form of a job offer she couldn't refuse.

Wesley had been the one left behind, trying to convince himself that six months of happiness was worth the devastation that followed.

Except Sloane wasn't Devon. Devon had never looked vulnerable. Had never needed a shield. Had never needed permission to believe that worth existed outside achievement.

Devon had used Millbrook Falls as a vacation from real life. Sloane was running from a real life that had imploded.

The difference mattered.

Maybe.

AT BEA'S COTTAGE, Sloane turned to him before getting out of her car. "Thank you. For today. For showing me... what you do."

"Verdict?"

"Your methods are still inefficient and probably give your business professor nightmares." She paused. "But they work. I can see why your patients love you."

"High praise from the spreadsheet queen."

"Don't get cocky. I might changed my mind."

"Already composing victory speech number two." Wesley grinned. "Same time tomorrow? Bea's session?"

"I'll be here."

As she walked toward the cottage, Wesley called after her. "Hey, Sloane?"

She turned.

"That rejection email at lunch? Their loss. Genuinely."

Something flickered across her face—vulnerability, quickly hidden. "Thanks."

He waited until she was inside before pulling out his phone.

Cora had texted: *How'd it go?*

Wesley stared at his phone, trying to figure out how to explain that he'd spent the day falling harder for someone who was absolutely, definitely, 100% leaving.

Finally he typed: *I'm screwed.*

Cora's response was immediate: *Yeah. I know.*

INSIDE, Bea was waiting with a sympathetic expression.

"How was your day of observation?"

"Educational." Sloane dropped onto the sofa. "He's good at what he does."

"And?"

"And nothing. He's a good physical therapist who makes terrible puns and probably shouldn't be allowed to choose his own scrubs."

"Mmm." Bea's smile was insufferable. "That's why you've been gone nine hours and came back looking like you've been hit by lightning."

"I don't look—"

"Darling, I spent forty years on stage. I know what people look like when they're falling in love."

"I'm not falling in love. I'm professionally acknowledging his competence."

"Of course you are." Bea settled back with obvious satisfaction. "Though you might want to tell your face that. It's been smiling for the past three minutes straight."

Sloane touched her face reflexively. Damn it. She had been smiling.

"He's temporary," she said, testing the words. "I mean, I'm temporary. Vermont's temporary. This is all temporary."

"Everything's temporary, dear. The question is whether you're going to enjoy it while it lasts or waste the whole time worrying about when it ends."

Sloane's phone buzzed. A text from Wesley: *PS - that was smile number twelve today. Personal record. I'm very proud of you.*

Despite everything—her career uncertainty, her savings dwindling, her mother's warnings echoing in her head—Sloane smiled.

Number thirteen.

CHAPTER 4

The diner appeared exactly as Sloane expected small-town Vermont to look: weathered building, hand-painted sign reading Maple & Main, and a parking lot that was basically a pickup truck convention. Plus one John Deere tractor. Today Wesley had tricked her into hanging out again. New people, he'd said. Making connections. Like she needed connections in Millbrook Falls. But sitting and waiting for the next rejection email was worse than hanging out with him.

"We're stopping for coffee?" she asked as Wesley pulled into a spot.

"Community coffee break. Happens every Wednesday." He held the door for her. "Good chance to catch up with patients, answer questions, remind people I exist."

The interior matched her expectations—vinyl booths that had seen better decades, laminate countertops, walls plastered with high school sports photos and community announcements. The air smelled like maple syrup and bacon and coffee that had been on the burner since approximately 1987.

"Wesley!" A woman behind the counter waved a coffee pot in greeting. "Your usual?"

"Thanks, Donna." Wesley turned to Sloane. "What would you like?"

"Black coffee, please."

Donna's sharp eyes traveled from Wesley to Sloane and back. "Don't think I've seen you around before."

"This is Sloane Hartwell," Wesley said quickly. "She's staying with Bea Kinsley while helping with her recovery."

"Bea's niece?" Donna's friendliness cooled noticeably. "Heard you were from Boston."

"Yes." Sloane accepted the mug Donna set down with slightly more force than necessary.

Wesley guided her to a booth near the window, either oblivious to the social dynamics or just used to them.

"So this is part of your practice?" Sloane kept her voice low. "Sitting in diners?"

"Community medicine." Wesley waved at an elderly couple across the room. "People feel more comfortable asking health questions in familiar settings. Plus, I learn things here I'd never get in a clinical environment."

As if to prove his point, a weathered farmer approached to ask about his wife's hip pain. Wesley listened, asked three specific questions, suggested a reevaluation.

The entire conversation took four minutes, but Sloane watched the man's shoulders relax with visible relief.

"You're providing free consultations during your coffee break," Sloane observed.

"I'm maintaining relationships." Wesley's coffee looked more like cream with coffee flavoring. "Makes people more likely to seek care when they need it."

Before Sloane could respond, a woman slid into the booth beside Wesley—early forties, professionally dressed, assessing eyes.

"Wesley Nakamura, are you finally dating someone?" Her gaze fixed on Sloane with undisguised curiosity. "Because the betting pool at the hospital has been running for two years."

Wesley's ears turned pink. "Sloane's a colleague, Karen. She's helping coordinate care for one of my patients."

"Uh-huh." Karen extended her hand. "Karen Fitzpatrick, emergency department nurse. I've known Wesley since he moved here five years ago."

Sloane shook her hand, noting the firm grip. "Sloane Hartwell."

"Bea's niece from the city, right? Only here temporarily." Karen's tone was pleasant but pointed. "Must be quite an adjustment from Boston."

"I'm managing."

Karen's smile didn't reach her eyes. It made her look like some kind of robot without the emotions behind the action. "So, that's your BMW? We don't see many luxury vehicles here. Mostly practical transportation—things that handle mud season and winter roads."

You don't belong here, was the unspoken message.

"I'm sure Sloane's car handles Vermont roads just fine," Wesley said with unexpected edge.

"Of course." Karen stood, patting Wesley's shoulder. "Just saying, city folks usually find rural life limiting. Most people from big cities can't wait to get back to civilization." She smiled at Sloane. "Enjoy your temporary visit to our little town."

After Karen left, Sloane waited a beat. "Well. That was subtle."

"Give them time." Wesley looked uncomfortable. "Small towns are protective. They've seen outsiders make promises and disappear."

"I never promised anything."

"You told Bea you're here until she recovers." Wesley's

voice was matter-of-fact. "Then back to your career. In a town this size, that information travels."

Sloane felt heat rise in her face. "So I'm being preemptively rejected?"

"You're being observed." He held her gaze. "People here have been burned by temporary helpers who left when things got boring. Why should they treat you differently?"

The words stung because they were fair. She *was* planning to leave. Had applications out in three different cities. Was here because she had nowhere else to go, not because she'd chosen this place.

And everyone knew it.

Wesley check to make sure Karen was definitely gone before speaking again.

"I'm sorry about that. Karen means well, but she's protective of the practice. And maybe a little too invested in my dating life."

Sloane's curiosity got the better of her. "Your dating life?"

Wesley looked uncomfortable but tried to joke. "Dating life is a strong term. More like people Karen thinks I should date."

"That's not what she meant."

"No." He sobered, running a hand through his hair. "There was someone. Devon. She came here for a summer residency, stayed six months, made a lot of promises about maybe building a life here."

Sloane waited, watching emotions flicker across his usually sunny face.

"Then she got a job offer in Boston. Left like Millbrook Falls had been a charming vacation rental." Wesley's smile was rueful. "So yeah, the town's cautious about temporary people. But that's my baggage, not your problem." He brightened deliberately. "Want to hear my Devon-related puns? They're terrible. Really scraping the bottom of the barrel—"

"I'm sorry," Sloane interrupted. "That she hurt you. And I'm sorry I'm... also temporary."

Wesley met her eyes. "The difference is, you're honest about it. You're not pretending this is anything other than what it is." He paused. "Also, you make better sarcastic comments. Devon was more passive-aggressive. You're actively aggressive. It's refreshing."

Despite everything, Sloane almost laughed. "That's a weird compliment."

"I'm a weird guy." His grin returned, though something vulnerable lingered in his eyes. "You might have noticed."

JACOB ORLAND SQUEEZED into their booth to ask about his back, forcing Sloane to slide closer to Wesley. Much closer.

Their thighs pressed together. Heat radiated between them. Neither moved away.

Wesley tried to focus on Jacob's question about lifting techniques for seed sacks, but every shift Sloane made sent awareness shooting through his nervous system. She smelled like something clean and expensive—probably some corporate brand that cost more than his weekly grocery budget.

His hand rested on the table, inches from hers. He watched her fingers toy with her coffee mug, hyperaware of the small distance between them.

"This is cozy," Sloane said quietly, not looking at him.

Wesley's voice came out lower than intended. "Too cozy?"

"I didn't say that."

He shifted slightly closer—they were basically pressed together now. "Good. Because I'm not moving."

Jacob finished his story and left. They had space now. Could separate. Neither moved.

Watching her try to hide devastation behind professional composure broke something in Wesley. This woman who organized chaos and color-coded her life couldn't control the one thing that mattered most to her identity.

The urge to make it better, to use every connection he had to find her opportunities, warred with the knowledge that she didn't want rescue. She wanted her competence recognized.

But a terrible, selfish part of him was glad those Boston firms kept rejecting her. Every "no" meant more time before she left. More mornings watching her frown at patient files. More chances to make her smile.

He was absolutely going to hell for that thought.

"We could stay like this," Wesley said. "For efficiency."

Sloane turned to look at him, eyebrow raised. "That's not how efficiency works."

"I'm learning from you. Redefining terms to suit my needs."

She bumped his shoulder, still not pulling away. "That's not learning. That's chaos."

"Chaotic learning. Very holistic."

She was smiling now, unable to help it. Wesley counted that as smile number—what was he up to? Seventeen? Eighteen?

He was keeping actual count. Which was pathetic. But also kind of his brand now.

THEY SPENT another hour at the diner, Wesley fielding questions from locals while Sloane observed. The way he moved through the community, how everyone seemed to know him, trust him.

She'd spent eight years building professional credibility through credentials and presentations and billable hours. Wesley had built his through showing up. Being present. Making terrible puns until people couldn't help but love him.

Different approaches to the same goal: mattering to someone.

Her phone buzzed. Yet another rejection email—from a firm she'd really wanted.

Thank you for your interest. After careful consideration, we've decided to move forward with other candidates...

The familiar words blurred. Thirty-eight rejections. She'd received thirty-eight professional rejections since being downsized.

THE AFTERNOON PASSED in a blur of patient visits and community interactions. By four PM, dark clouds had rolled in over the mountains.

"We should head back," Wesley said, checking the sky. "Storm's coming."

They made it halfway to Bea's cottage before the sky opened up.

Rain hit the windshield like a wall. Visibility dropped to nearly zero in seconds. Wesley's truck slowed, pulled over.

Sloane followed, parking behind him. Within moments, she was drenched just running the few feet to his passenger door.

"Get in!" Wesley called.

She climbed into his truck, water dripping everywhere. "This is just a little rain."

"Atmospheric flash flood warning. Very dramatic. Very Vermont." But Wesley was checking his mirrors, assessing the road.

"Should we find higher ground—"

"Hey." He turned to face her fully. "We're safe here. I promise. This road doesn't flood."

"How do you know?"

"Because I've driven it in worse storms. Trust me."

Sloane took a shaky breath. "Trust. That thing I'm notoriously good at."

"You trusted me with Bea's care."

"That's different."

"Is it?" Wesley reached for her hand in the dim light. "You're letting me do my job my way. That's trust."

His hand was warm, solid. Real. Sloane found herself gripping it harder than she intended.

"I DON'T KNOW who I am without my career," Sloane admitted quietly. The darkness made it easier somehow. "Corporate consulting was supposed to be my whole life. And I lost it anyway."

Wesley's thumb traced circles on her palm. "I sometimes wonder if choosing contentment was brave or cowardly. If I gave up too easily on the prestige thing because I was scared I'd fail anyway."

"You didn't give up." Sloane turned to face him. "You chose differently. There's a difference."

"That's what I keep telling myself."

"Besides, your way is working. Bea's recovering. Your patients love you. You make terrible puns and people still hire you." She paused. "That's basically magic."

Wesley laughed, the sound warm in the enclosed space. "Was that a compliment? From the grump herself?"

"Don't let it go to your head, Sunshine."

His voice went soft. "You're brave, Sloane. Not a coward. You're scared. There's a difference."

She squeezed his hand. "When did you get wise?"

"I've always been wise. You were just too busy being organized to notice."

They sat like that, hands linked, rain pounding overhead.

Thunder rolled across the mountains. Lightning flickered in the distance.

Sloane should pull away. Should maintain professional distance. Should remember that she was leaving as soon as Bea recovered.

Instead, she tightened her grip.

WHEN THE RAIN finally eased to a manageable downpour, neither moved immediately.

"We should get you back to Bea," Wesley said.

"Probably."

But neither let go for another beat.

Wesley squeezed her hand once before releasing it. "Thanks for not panicking."

"Thanks for being annoyingly calm."

"It's my brand." He grinned. "Along with excellent puns and excessive optimism."

"Don't forget the finger guns."

"Never forget the finger guns." He demonstrated, making her laugh.

Sloane climbed out, ran back to her car through the rain. But something had shifted between them. The teasing covered something deeper now. Something real.

Something terrifying.

WESLEY WATCHED HER DRIVE AWAY, his hand still warm from holding hers.

I'm so screwed, he thought.

Not just falling for Sloane Hartwell. Already fallen. Past tense. Done deal.

For someone who'd made it crystal clear she was leaving.

Who had applications out in three cities. Who saw Millbrook Falls as a temporary stopping point between her real life.

Exactly like Devon.

Except not like Devon at all.

Devon had used Vermont as a vacation. Sloane was running from wreckage. The difference mattered.

Maybe.

His phone buzzed. Text from Cora: *How'd the rounds go?*

Wesley stared at the screen. How could he explain that he'd just held hands with someone who was definitely leaving while sitting in a rainstorm discussing their respective career failures?

Finally he typed: *I'm in so much trouble.*

Cora: *Define trouble.*

The falling-in-love-with-someone-temporary kind.

Three dots appeared. Disappeared. Appeared again.

Finally: *Shit. Wesley.*

I know.

Does she know?

That I'm falling for her? No. That she's falling for me? Also no. We're both very committed to ignoring it.

How's that working out?

Wesley looked at his hand, still feeling the ghost of her fingers intertwined with his.

Terribly. It's working terribly.

BACK AT BEA'S COTTAGE, Sloane sat in her car for a long moment, staring at nothing.

She'd held Wesley's hand.

In a rainstorm.

While discussing their deepest fears.

Like they were in some kind of romantic movie instead of real life where she had a career to rebuild and he had a practice to run and they were fundamentally incompatible in every way that mattered.

Her phone buzzed. Text from her former colleague: *Heard through grapevine that Morrison & Associates is hiring. Want me to put in a word?*

Morrison & Associates. Top-tier consulting firm. Chicago. Everything she'd been working toward.

Sloane stared at the message.

Six weeks ago, she would have responded immediately with an enthusiastic yes.

Now she found herself thinking about puns and community coffee breaks and the way Wesley's hand felt solid and warm in the darkness.

This is temporary, she reminded herself firmly. *He knows it's temporary. You know it's temporary. Everyone knows it's temporary.*

She typed back: *Yes please. Thanks for thinking of me.*

Then sat in her car, rain drumming on the roof, trying to convince herself she'd made the right choice.

Inside, Bea was waiting with hot tea and a hopeful expression. "How was your day?"

"Educational." Sloane wrapped her hands around the mug. "Wesley's practice is, well, pretty much what I saw on the first drive along. Different from what I though it would be."

"Different good or different bad?"

"Different complicated."

Bea smiled. "Ah. The best kind of different."

"I'm not staying, Aunt Bea. You know that, right? I'm here until you recover, then I'm going back to my real life."

"Of course, darling." Bea sipped her tea.

CHAPTER 5

Sloane woke at 5:47 AM to the sound of birds greeting the day. The dawn chorus, Bea said the first time she'd complained. Who knew that birds could be louder than traffic in the morning?

She'd spent the night tossing and turning, her mind stuck on yesterday's rainstorm. On Wesley's hand in hers. On the way he'd looked at her like she mattered, like her fear was valid but not insurmountable.

On the Morrison & Associates job offer she'd said yes to while wanting to say no.

Sleep was clearly not happening. Sloane pulled on running clothes, then changed her mind. Too much energy for running. Not enough coffee for existing.

She grabbed her tablet and a blanket, heading for the porch where she could pretend to be productive while actually just doom-scrolling job listings and questioning every life choice that had led her here.

The morning air was cool, smelling of dew and pine. Sloane wrapped the blanket around her shoulders and settled onto the porch steps with her coffee, watching the sun paint Mount Mansfield in shades of pink and gold.

This is nice, she admitted reluctantly. *Annoyingly nice.*

The sound of an engine broke the peaceful quiet. Wesley's disreputable Subaru turned into the driveway.

At 6:30 AM.

Sloane looked down at herself. Tank top. Sleep shorts. Hair in a messy bun with a million flyaways. No makeup. Probably pillow creases on her face.

Shit.

She started to stand, retreat inside, but Wesley was already out of the car with a bakery bag and that insufferable smile.

"I didn't know you did early sessions," she called, trying to sound casual instead of panicked.

Wesley stopped halfway up the path, staring. Just staring. "Sorry, I—wow. You look different."

Sloane crossed her arms over her chest. "Different?"

"Different beautiful." He seemed to catch himself, ears going pink. "I mean, you're always—I brought cinnamon rolls from the bakery. I'm going to stop talking now."

Despite everything, Sloane fought a smile. "Probably wise."

"Can I join you? Or is this your private brooding time?" Wesley held up the bag. "I have enough pastries to share. As a bribe for interrupting your solitude."

She should say no. Should go inside and put on armor—both literal and metaphorical. Should maintain professional boundaries.

Instead, she patted the step beside her. "I suppose brooding is better with cinnamon rolls."

. . .

WESLEY SAT DOWN, hyperaware of the bare skin of her shoulder inches from his arm. Sloane without her corporate armor was devastating. Her hair caught the morning light, and without makeup he could see a spray of freckles across her nose. She looked younger, less defended, and beautiful in a way that made his chest ache.

Also slightly grumpy about being seen without her armor, which was adorable.

He handed her a cinnamon roll, trying not to stare at the way morning light painted her skin gold.

"Couldn't sleep?" he asked.

"I kept thinking about what you said. About measuring the wrong things." She took a bite, closing her eyes. "It's annoyingly stuck in my head."

"My philosophical puns are finally working!"

"They're not puns if they're accidentally profound."

"I'll take accidental profundity. It's very on-brand for me." Wesley grinned through a mouthful of pastry. "What specifically is stuck?"

Sloane was quiet for a moment, watching the sunrise. "If I'm not measuring success by salary and title and office size... what else is there? I genuinely don't know."

"Happiness. Connection. Whether you wake up excited about your day."

"That sounds fake."

"It's not. But I get why it sounds that way when you're used to quantifiable metrics." Wesley shifted to face her more fully. "Can I ask you something?"

"You're going to anyway."

"True." He smiled. "When was the last time you woke up excited about your day? Not anxious, not determined to prove yourself. Actually excited."

Sloane opened her mouth, to answer and then didn't say

anything. Her brow furrowed in that way it did when she was genuinely thinking.

"I don't remember," she admitted finally. "Isn't that pathetic? Eight years of climbing the corporate ladder and I can't remember a single morning where I thought I can't wait for today."

"Do you wake up excited about your days?" She turned to look at him. "Really? Or is that just your relentless optimism talking?"

"Most days, yeah. Even the hard ones." Wesley gestured around them. "Even when Mrs. Patterson complains about my music choices and Hank argues about booth placement and my student loans remind me I'll never own a house."

"That sounds exhausting."

"It sounds like life." He bumped her shoulder gently with his. "You should try it sometime."

"Hard pass."

"Challenge accepted." Wesley took another bite of cinnamon roll, trying not to notice how close they were sitting. How her bare shoulder was right there, touchable.

The urge to lean in, to taste cinnamon on her lips, to pull her into his lap and show her she didn't need achievement to be worthy—it took every ounce of discipline to stay still.

She wasn't ready. Still measuring herself by those rejection emails, still convinced her value lived in a corporate office somewhere. Kissing her now would be taking advantage of her vulnerability.

Even if she was looking at him, like maybe she wanted him to.

"YOU HAVE FROSTING ON YOUR NOSE," Wesley said, his voice going softer.

Before Sloane could react, he reached out, his thumb

brushing the tip of her nose. The touch was gentle, fleeting, but it sent electricity straight down her spine.

"There. Perfect."

Sloane's voice came out embarrassingly husky. "Perfect is a strong word."

"I stand by it." His thumb lingered on her cheek, just for a second.

The moment stretched between them, charged with everything they weren't saying. The morning sounds—birds, waterfall, distant traffic—faded to white noise.

Wesley's phone buzzed.

They both jumped back, laughing nervously.

"Duty calls." Wesley checked his screen, grimacing. "Mrs. Patterson's hip is acting up. Emergency session."

"Of course it is." Sloane wasn't sure if she was relieved or disappointed.

Wesley stood, offering his hand to help her up. "But Sloane? This—" He gestured between them. "—we should talk about this."

She took his hand, felt his fingers close warm and strong around hers. "There's nothing to talk about."

"You're a terrible liar for someone who worked in corporate consulting."

"Fine." Sloane stood but didn't let go immediately. "Maybe there's something. But I don't know what to do with something."

"We could start with admitting it exists."

"It might exist. Provisionally."

"I'll take provisional." Wesley squeezed her hand and the let it go. "See you at Bea's session?"

"Unfortunately."

"You mean fortunately."

"I meant what I said."

But she was smiling, and they both knew she was lying.

. . .

After Bea's morning session, Wesley asked if Sloane wanted to visit the fairgrounds to assess the wellness fair setup.

"I thought you said you didn't need my organizational skills," Sloane said.

"I said I didn't need you to micromanage Bea's recovery. I absolutely need your organizational skills for a community event run by volunteers who think planning ahead means showing up the day before."

"That's terrifying."

"Welcome to small-town event management." Wesley grinned. "Bring your color-coded spreadsheets. We're going to need them."

The Millbrook Falls Fairgrounds looked like someone had designed a venue specifically to give Sloane organizational anxiety.

No clear pathways. Vendor booths scattered randomly. What appeared to be a petting zoo in the middle of where the wellness demonstrations were supposed to happen.

"This is chaos," Sloane said.

"This is Vermont." Wesley was already walking toward a cluster of people arguing over a hand-drawn map. "Come on, let's meet the committee."

The Wellness Fair Planning Committee consisted of: Hank, a farmer who seemed personally offended by the concept of change. Margot, a yoga instructor who wanted more intentional energy flow. Cordelia, Bea's friend, an elderly woman who kept referring to how we did it in 98. And three others whose names Sloane immediately forgot.

"This is Sloane Hartwell," Wesley introduced. "Bea's niece. She's agreed to help with logistics and organization."

Hank squinted at her. "You're the city woman. In the BMW."

"That's me." Sloane refused to be defensive about her car.

"What do you know about community fairs?"

"Nothing. But I know about organizational systems, efficient resource allocation, and preventing logistical disasters." Sloane pulled out her tablet. "Which, from what I can see, you're going to need."

For the next hour, Sloane watched the committee argue about booth placement, vendor selection, and whether the goat yoga demonstration counted as wellness or entertainment.

Wesley stood beside her, close enough that their arms brushed occasionally.

"You're doing that on purpose," Sloane muttered during a particularly heated debate about parking.

"Doing what?"

"Walking too close. You have the entire fairground."

"Maybe I like being close to you." Wesley's grin was unrepentant.

She glared at him. "Smooth."

"I thought so. I've been practicing."

When Sloane stumbled on uneven ground, Wesley caught her elbow, steadying her. His hand lingered.

"Thanks. You can let go now."

"Can I? The ground is very uneven. Safety first."

"Wesley."

"Fine." But he was grinning.

WATCHING SLOANE WORK WAS MESMERIZING.

She listened to Hank's concerns about vendor fees, then

suggested a tiered pricing system that accommodated local businesses while covering costs. When Margot wanted to eliminate the beer garden for being "spiritually incongruent," Sloane proposed separating wellness and entertainment zones to create distinct experiences.

This was Sloane at her best—sharp mind balanced with genuine respect for others' expertise. She didn't bulldoze; she listened and adapted.

His chest swelled with something dangerously close to pride. She was magnificent.

The urge to put his arm around her, to claim her in front of these people, caught him off guard. She wasn't his. Wouldn't be his. But damn if he didn't want—

"Earth to Wesley," Margot said. "I asked if you wanted to share the water bottle?"

Wesley snapped back to reality. Margot was offering their communal water bottle, but Sloane was right there, looking slightly flushed from the heat.

"Actually—" Wesley handed it to Sloane. "Thirsty?"

She hesitated, staring at the bottle like it might bite her. "That's..."

"Unhygienic? Probably. But we're adults. We can handle shared water bottles."

Sloane took it, maintaining eye contact while drinking. "There. Happy?"

Wesley's voice came out rougher than intended. "Getting there."

THEY STOOD CLOSE LOOKING at the same map, Wesley leaning over her shoulder to point out the main stage location.

"If we move the wellness demo here—"

Sloane could barely focus on the map. His warmth at her

back, his breath stirring her hair, the scent of his shampoo—it was all too much and not enough.

"That's... fine. Whatever you think."

Wesley noticed her distraction. "You okay? You seem flustered."

"I'm not flustered."

"You're blushing."

"That's sun exposure."

"It's 9 AM and we're in the shade."

After two hours, they'd created a basic layout that satisfied most of the committee. Cordelia was still muttering about '98, but everyone else seemed cautiously optimistic.

"You two work well together," Margot observed, smiling. "How long have you been dating?"

"We're not—" Sloane started.

"We're just—" Wesley said at the same time.

"Professional colleagues!" they said in unison.

Margot's smile turned knowing. "Uh-huh. Keep telling yourselves that. But just so you know, the betting pool has you two together by the end of the fair."

She walked away, leaving them in awkward silence.

"Betting pool?" Sloane asked.

"Small towns." Wesley shrugged. "They have nothing better to do."

"Should we be worried?"

"About the betting pool or about the fact that they might be right?"

Sloane looked at him sharply. "Wesley—"

"I'm kidding. Mostly. Maybe." He grinned, but something serious lingered in his eyes. "Come on, let's go annoy Hank with optimization suggestions."

But for the rest of the morning, Sloane kept catching Wesley looking at her. And he kept catching her looking back.

. . .

Later that afternoon, Sloane followed Wesley back to his clinic to help him catch up on paperwork.

"You don't have to do this," Wesley said, unlocking the door.

"I know. But if I go back to Bea's, I'll just obsessively refresh my email checking for rejections." Sloane followed him inside. "At least here I can organize your filing system and pretend to be useful."

"My filing system is fine."

"I'd bet big money your filing system is held together by hope and outdated sticky notes." But she was smiling.

They worked in comfortable silence, Wesley making notes on patient files while Sloane reorganized his cabinets with terrifying efficiency. The afternoon sun slanted through the windows, painting everything gold.

Wesley found himself watching Sloane more than his paperwork. The concentration on her face, the way she bit her lower lip when thinking, the satisfaction when she found the perfect organizational solution.

Her hands were distracting—capable and sure, moving through files with the same precision she brought to everything.

"What?" Sloane caught him staring.

The words came out before Wesley could stop them: "You have nice hands."

Sloane blinked. "What?"

"I mean—" Heat crawled up his neck. "That was weird. Sorry. Professional observation. Very professional."

Sloane looked at the skin she'd been abusing for hours handling paper. "They are just hands. Look at the paper cuts.

I need a manicure. Anyway, yours are nice too." Why was she babbling?

Wesley stood, moving closer. "You think I have nice hands?"

"I meant professionally. They're very... therapeutic. Therapeutically nice."

"Therapeutic hands. That's what we're calling it?"

"Don't make it weird."

"I'm not making it weird." Wesley took another step. "You're making it weird by trying to take it back."

They were close now. Too close. Sloane could see the gold flecks in his brown eyes, count his heartbeats in the pulse at his throat.

"What would you call it, then?" Wesley's voice was soft.

Sloane met his eyes, defiant despite her racing heart. "Dangerous."

"Dangerous how?"

"Like I might do something stupid if you get any closer."

Wesley stopped, respecting her boundary, but his eyes were dark with something that made her breath catch. "Stupid good or stupid bad?"

"Both. Definitely both." Sloane gripped the edge of the desk.

"For the record?" Wesley said. "Even with the cuts, I think your hands are great."

Sloane blinked. "What?"

"The way you organize things. It's like watching an artist. Very competent hands."

"That's ridiculous."

"Is it? Because you just complimented my hands and I'm returning the favor." Wesley grinned. "I also think you're beautiful when you're grumpy. Which is most of the time. So that works out well for me."

She was flustered now, color high in her cheeks. "You can't just say things like that."

"Why not? It's true." He took one more step, close enough to touch. "You're blushing again. It's cute."

"I don't do cute."

"You're doing it right now."

The air between them felt charged, electric. Wesley could see the way her breath had gone shallow.

One more step and he could kiss her. One more step and—

His phone rang.

They both jumped back like they'd been caught doing something wrong.

"Sorry, I—" Wesley pulled out his phone. Patient emergency. Of course. "I have to take this."

Sloane nodded, not quite meeting his eyes.

Wesley stepped into his office for the call, and when he came back out five minutes later, Sloane was gathering her things.

"I should go. Let you handle the emergency."

"Sloane, wait." He caught her hand. "We should talk about this. The hands thing. The dangerous thing. All of it."

She finally met his eyes. "I don't know what to say."

"Then don't say anything yet. Just... don't run away from it, okay?"

Sloane squeezed his hand once. "I'll try."

After she left, Wesley sat at his desk, running his fingers through his hair.

His phone buzzed. Text from Cora: *How's the not-falling-for-her thing going?*

Wesley stared at the ceiling. *Do you have a camera in here? Terribly. It's going terribly.*

Called it.

You're not helping.

I'm being supportive from a distance while you make poor life choices. It's what friends do.

Wesley smiled despite himself. *She complimented my hands.*

... What?

Long story. But it was adorable.

You're doomed.

I know.

SLOANE SAT in her car outside the clinic for a full five minutes, trying to remember how to breathe normally.

She'd complimented his hands. Out loud. Like some kind of romance novel character having a moment.

And he'd said she was beautiful when she was grumpy.

And they'd almost kissed. Again.

Her phone buzzed. Email from Morrison & Associates: *We'd love to schedule a preliminary phone interview for next week. Are you available Tuesday at 2 PM?*

Six weeks ago, this would have been everything she wanted. Top-tier firm, Chicago, exactly the kind of position she'd been working toward her entire career.

Now she found herself thinking about terrible puns and cinnamon rolls and the way Wesley stared at her like she was worth more than her resume.

This is temporary, she reminded herself. *He knows it. You know it. Everyone knows it.*

She typed back: *Tuesday at 2 PM works perfectly. Thank you for the opportunity.*

Then sat in the parking lot, fighting the urge to call back and cancel.

Inside Bea's cottage, her aunt was waiting with tea. "How was your day?"

"Productive." Sloane took the mug. "We made progress on the wellness fair layout."

"And?"

"And nothing. Wesley's very good at community coordination."

"Mmm." Bea's smile was insufferable. "That's why you've been sitting in your car for ten minutes looking like you just survived a natural disaster?"

"I was making phone calls."

"Of course you were, darling." Bea sipped her tea.

CHAPTER 6

The heat wave hit on Tuesday.

By Wednesday morning, Millbrook Falls felt like someone had opened an oven door and forgotten to close it. The air conditioning in Wesley's clinic wheezed like it was on life support, barely managing to lower the temperature from "unbearable" to "merely oppressive."

Sloane had dressed for the heat—lightweight cotton blouse, shorts, her hair pulled up off her neck. She was helping Wesley reorganize patient files while he caught up on documentation.

She was not prepared for Wesley in a tank top.

The clinic dress code apparently relaxed during heat waves, because Wesley had shown up in scrubs pants and a plain black tank top that left his arms and shoulders completely exposed. Arms that were more defined than any physical therapist had a right to be. Shoulders that flexed and moved under golden skin every time he reached for a file or leaned over to write notes.

Sloane tried to focus on alphabetizing. Failed miserably.

This was unprofessional. She was helping with Bea's care,

job hunting, planning a temporary existence. She couldn't afford to want Wesley Nakamura's hands on her body.

But her body wasn't listening.

Every time he leaned over her shoulder to check her work, heat pooled low in her belly. Every casual touch—passing files, reaching for the same cabinet—sent electricity through her nerves.

This was getting out of control.

"You okay?" Wesley asked, looking up from his notes. "You seem distracted."

Because you're essentially shirtless and I'm trying to remember why this is a bad idea, Sloane thought.

"I'm fine," she said. "Just hot."

"The AC is losing the battle." Wesley pulled his water bottle from the mini fridge, pressing it against his neck. Condensation dripped down his skin.

Sloane looked away quickly. "Maybe we should work on Bea's treatment plan instead. Something that requires less... proximity."

"Less proximity?" Wesley's eyebrow rose, amusement in his voice. "Are we too close, Sloane?"

Yes. No. Maybe. Help.

"I just think we could be more efficient if we had separate tasks."

"Efficient." Wesley set down his water bottle, moving closer instead of farther away. "Is that what's bothering you? Efficiency?"

"What else would it be?"

"I don't know. You tell me." He was close now, close enough that she could see a bead of sweat trailing down his collarbone. "You've been jumping every time I get near you. You can barely look at me. And you just suggested we work separately despite spending the last three days insisting on collaborative planning."

Sloane's heart hammered. "I'm not—"

"You're not what? Not completely aware of me? Not thinking about—" He stopped himself. "Never mind."

"Not thinking about what?"

Wesley held her gaze. "Things we probably shouldn't be thinking about in a professional setting."

Forget the setting. We shouldn't be thinking about anything. Sloane's mouth went dry.

"I don't know what you're talking about."

"Liar." But Wesley's voice was gentle. "You're a terrible liar, remember?"

WORKING this close to Sloane in the heat was torture.

She'd pulled her hair up, exposing the elegant line of her neck, and Wesley couldn't stop imagining what she'd taste like if he pressed his mouth to that pulse point. The lightweight blouse she wore did nothing to hide the shape of her, and when she'd bent over the filing cabinet earlier, her shirt riding up to expose a strip of skin at her lower back, he'd actually bit his tongue to keep from making a sound.

Boundaries were crumbling. He didn't care if she was temporary. The pain when she left wouldn't be any different whether he kissed her or not.

The way she watched him, pupils dilated and breath quickening when they got close—she wanted this as much as he did. The question was whether either of them would be brave enough to admit it.

"We should talk about this," Wesley said.

"About what?" Sloane was backing toward the door.

"About the fact that you're considering running away right now."

"I'm not running—"

"Sloane." He stepped closer. "What are you afraid of?"

. . .

"I'M NOT AFRAID OF ANYTHING." But even to her own ears, the denial sounded weak.

"Really? Because you're white-knuckling that file folder like it's the only thing keeping you upright."

Sloane looked down. Damn it. She was gripping the folder hard enough to crumple it.

"Your approach is chaos," she said, changing tactics. "No metrics, no accountability. How do you know you're actually helping people?"

"This isn't about patient care." Wesley's voice was quiet, steady. "What are you really afraid of?"

Something in Sloane snapped.

"I'm afraid of staying!" The words exploded out of her. "Okay? I'm afraid that if I stop planning my exit strategy for five minutes, I'll wake up in six months having forgotten I had a career. Having forgotten who I was supposed to be. Having—"

She stopped herself, but it was too late.

Wesley's voice was barely above a whisper. "Having what? Having fallen for a small-town physical therapist who thinks contentment is enough?"

Neither of them could speak. They'd been avoiding too many things.

"I can't afford this, Wesley." Sloane's voice shook. "Any of this. This town, these feelings, you—I can't afford to want things I can't keep."

He moved closer. "Who says you can't keep them?"

"Me. I say I can't." The words came out rough, raw. "Because I watched my mother waste her potential on a man who left. Because I've spent eight years building a career that vanished overnight. Because staying here means admitting I failed at the life I was supposed to have."

Wesley's expression softened. "Or maybe it means succeeding at a life you didn't know you wanted."

"That's easy for you to say. You chose this. I didn't choose unemployment. I didn't choose Vermont. I didn't choose—" She gestured between them. "This."

"Didn't you?" Wesley moved closer still until they were barely a foot apart. "Because from where I'm standing, you've been choosing this every day. Every morning you show up for Bea's sessions. Every afternoon you help with my practice. Every moment you stay instead of leaving."

"That's not—"

"That's not what? Not choosing? Not wanting?" His voice dropped lower. "Not feeling exactly what I'm feeling?"

Wesley lifted his hand toward her face, slowly enough that she could step away.

She didn't step away.

His fingers brushed her jaw, and Sloane's eyes fluttered closed.

"We shouldn't," she whispered.

"No," Wesley agreed. But he didn't move away. Couldn't move away.

Her hands fisted in his tank top, pulling him closer even as she protested.

"This is a terrible idea," she said.

"Absolutely terrible." Wesley's thumb traced the line of her jaw, watching goosebumps rise on her skin despite the heat.

Their lips were inches apart. He could feel her breath on his mouth, could see the war between want and fear in her eyes.

"Sloane," he started.

The clinic door swung open.

"Oh my!" Cordelia Ashworth stood in the doorway, immaculate in linen despite the heat, her expression delighted. "Did I interrupt something?"

Wesley and Sloane jumped apart like they'd been electrocuted.

"We were just—" Sloane started.

"Discussing patient files," Wesley finished lamely.

"So close together," Cordelia observed, eyes twinkling. "How... intense."

Sloane's face burned. "I should check on Bea."

She fled before anyone could stop her, leaving her tablet, her notes, and what was left of her dignity behind.

Outside, the heat hit her like a wall, but it was nothing compared to the fire still burning through her system. She'd almost kissed him. Had been seconds away from pulling Wesley Nakamura into her arms and showing him that she didn't care about professional boundaries or temporary status or any of the very good reasons they shouldn't—

Her phone rang. Morrison & Associates.

Right. The interview. The job. The real life waiting for her back in civilization.

"Hello, this is Sloane Hartwell."

"Ms. Hartwell, this is Jennifer Aden from Morrison & Associates. We hoped we could move your interview forward by a day. Can you come on Monday?"

Monday. Five days from now.

"Yes," Sloane heard herself say. "Monday works perfectly."

She hung up and stared at her phone.

INSIDE THE CLINIC, Cordelia settled into a chair with the air of someone who had no demands on her time.

"That young woman," she said, "is terrified of happiness."

Wesley ran his hands through his hair. "I know."

"Are you brave enough to wait for her to get over her fear?"

"I don't know." Wesley sank into his desk chair. "What if she never does?"

"Then you'll have your answer." Cordelia's voice was gentle but firm. "But I don't think that's the question you're really asking."

"What am I really asking?"

"You're asking if loving someone who might leave is worth the risk again." Cordelia stood, collecting her purse. "And only you can answer that, dear boy. Though for what it's worth, I think she's asking herself the same question."

After Cordelia left, Wesley sat at his desk for a long time, staring at nothing.

He'd almost kissed her. Had been seconds away from pulling Sloane Hartwell into his arms and showing her that contentment and passion weren't mutually exclusive. That choosing a different kind of success didn't mean settling for less.

But she'd been right about the timing. She was still grieving her career, still trying to figure out who she was without the corporate identity. If he kissed her right now, he'd feel like he was taking advantage. Something he never wanted to do.

He'd wait. Give her space to find her footing.

And hope that when she did, she'd turn toward him instead of away.

His phone buzzed. Text from Sloane: *I won't be able to help at the clinic. Need to prepare for an interview in Chicago.*

Wesley stared at the message.

Five days. He had five days before she left for an interview that could take her away permanently. Five days to prove she belonged here.

He typed back: *Congratulations. You'll be great.*

What he wanted to say was *Don't go. Stay here. Give us a chance.*

But Sloane needed to make her own choices. Needed to figure out what she wanted without pressure from someone who was falling in love with her.

Even if it killed him to let her go.

BACK AT BEA'S COTTAGE, Sloane found her aunt on the porch with iced tea and a twinkle in her eyes. "Cordelia texted me," Bea said. "Said you left the clinic rather suddenly."

"She walked in at an inopportune moment."

"Inopportune." Bea's smile was insufferable. "Is that what we're calling it?"

"We weren't—" Sloane stopped. "Nothing happened."

"But something almost happened."

Sloane sank into the chair beside her aunt. "I got an interview request. Chicago. Monday."

"Congratulations, darling. That's wonderful news."

"Is it?" Sloane pulled her knees up to her chest. "Because it doesn't feel wonderful. It feels like I'm running away from the first real thing I've felt in eight years. And you still need me."

Bea gave her a theatrical shrug. "Then maybe you shouldn't go."

"I have to go. This is my career. My life. My plan."

"Your plan." Bea sipped her tea. "The same plan that had you miserable in Boston, working eighty-hour weeks, measuring your worth by your salary?"

"That plan was working until I got laid off."

"Was it, though? You never called unless you were between deals. You never visited. You sent gift cards for my birthday instead of showing up." Bea's voice was gentle but pointed. "You were succeeding at a life that made you lonely and exhausted. Is that really what you want back?"

Sloane didn't have an answer.

Her phone buzzed. Wesley's response: *Congratulations. You'll be great.*

Short. Professional. Exactly what it should be.

So why did it feel like goodbye?

WESLEY WAS STILL at the clinic at 10 PM, pretending to do paperwork while actually just sitting in the dark thinking about Sloane.

His phone rang. Cora.

"You're still at the clinic, aren't you?"

"How did you know?"

"Because you only work late when you're avoiding something." Cora's voice was sympathetic. "What happened?"

"I almost kissed her. Then Cordelia walked in. Then Sloane got a job interview in Chicago and is flying out Sunday."

"Shit."

"Yeah."

"Are you going to tell her how you feel?"

Wesley stared at the ceiling. "How I feel? That watching her leave is going to destroy me but I still want every minute I can get before she goes?"

"Yes. That."

"No." Wesley scrubbed his hands over his face. "Because she needs to make this choice without pressure. Without feeling like she owes me anything or has to choose between her dreams and... whatever this is between us."

"Wesley."

"I know it's stupid. But I can't be the reason she stays. If she stays, it has to be because she wants this life. Not because she feels obligated to someone who couldn't keep his feelings in control."

Cora was quiet for a long moment. "You're going to regret this."

"Probably." Wesley smiled sadly. "But at least I'll regret letting her go freely instead of regret trying to hold her back."

"That's very noble and very stupid."

"It's my brand."

After hanging up, Wesley sat in the darkness, trying to memorize what it felt like to be this close to happy before it slipped away.

He had five days.

Five days to not fall any deeper in love with Sloane Hartwell.

It was already too late.

CHAPTER 7

It had been three days since the almost-kiss in Wesley's clinic, and Sloane was losing her mind.

She'd tried avoiding him. Tried staying professional. Tried convincing herself that the interview in Chicago was what she wanted.

All of it failed spectacularly when Bea insisted Sloane needed to be present for the morning therapy session.

"I might need help," Bea said innocently. "With the... positioning."

Bea was under the illusion she was being subtle. "You've been doing these new exercises for two weeks."

"Humor an old woman, darling."

So Sloane found herself on the porch when Wesley arrived at exactly 9 AM, looking insufferably cheerful despite the rain.

"Morning! Beautiful day for therapy!"

Sloane gestured at the downpour. "It's raining."

"Perfect weather for indoor healing!" Wesley was practically bouncing as he set up his equipment.

"You're insufferable before coffee."

"I had three cups. I'm very energized."

"That explains so much."

Bea watched their exchange with undisguised delight before suddenly announcing, "Oh my, I need to use the facilities. This might take a while. You two carry on without me."

She disappeared inside, leaving Sloane and Wesley alone on the porch.

Rain drummed on the roof. Awkward silence stretched between them.

Wesley started humming while organizing his therapy equipment.

"Can you not?" Sloane said.

"Not what?"

"The humming. The cheerfulness. The existing."

He grinned at her. "Someone woke up extra grumpy today."

"I'm always this grumpy. You're just noticing now?"

"Oh, I noticed. I'm cataloging your grumpiness levels. Today's a solid eight out of ten."

Despite herself, Sloane was curious. "What's a ten?"

"Before coffee and when I'm being particularly optimistic."

"So basically every morning?"

"Exactly! See, you're learning my patterns." Wesley's smile softened. "We should probably talk about what almost happened."

Sloane's heart kicked up. The last thing she wanted to do was talk about that. Ignoring it would be the best. "The clinic thing?"

He looked at her out of the corner of his eyes as he laid out the bands for Bea's session. "Yeah. That."

"Should we? Or should we pretend boundaries still exist?"

"Do they?" Wesley set down his equipment, giving her his full attention. "Exist, I mean?"

Why couldn't he just let it go. Probably the same reason can't no matter how hard I try. "I don't know. Do they?"

"Not for me." His voice was quiet but steady. "Not anymore. I think about you constantly, which is very inconvenient for patient focus."

Where was Bea? "That's unprofessional."

"I know. But I'm done pretending." Wesley held her gaze. "Are you?"

Before Sloane could answer—before she could figure out what the hell she wanted to say—Wesley's phone rang.

He checked it, grimacing. "Mrs. Patterson. Her hip is acting up again." He looked at Sloane apologetically. "I'll reschedule Bea. Her progress is great. Mrs. P is in a lot of pain."

"Go. We'll talk later."

"Later," Wesley agreed. "Definitely later."

But his eyes said he wasn't sure later would ever come.

THE DAY WENT from bad to catastrophic around noon.

Wesley was in the middle of a session when he heard a terrible grinding noise followed by an ominous silence.

The air conditioning had died.

Within fifteen minutes, the clinic felt like a sauna. Within thirty, his patients were wilting. By the time his afternoon appointments arrived, the temperature had climbed to ninety-five degrees inside.

"I'm so sorry," Wesley told Mrs. Williams, his 2 PM. "I can reschedule—"

"Nonsense. I'm here, you're here. We'll manage." But she was fanning herself with a magazine.

Wesley's phone rang. Sloane.

"I heard the AC died," she said without preamble. "Do you need help?"

"I can't ask you to—"

"You didn't ask. I'm offering. I called three HVAC companies. Earliest anyone can come is tomorrow. But I can help. Bring fans, or ice, or both. I can call patients to warn them, whatever you need."

Wesley felt something warm bloom in his chest. "I thought you were avoiding me?"

"I'm very good during disasters. It's kind of my thing."

"Get over here. Please."

BY THREE PM, Sloane had transformed Wesley's disaster into just uncomfortable.

She'd rescheduled the patients who couldn't handle the heat, set up fans in every corner, created a rotation system so people could cool down in their cars between exercises. She'd run to the store for ice water and sports drinks, fielded phone calls, and somehow kept Wesley on schedule.

They worked side by side, passing water bottles, steadying patients, reaching for the same supplies. Every touch sent awareness shooting through her system, but there was no time to process it. Only time to move to the next crisis.

"You're amazing at this," Wesley said during a brief break.

"At crisis management? It's literally what I was trained for."

"No. At caring about people you just met. At seeing what needs to be done and doing it." He was looking at her with something in his eyes that made her breath catch. "You belong here, Sloane. In this work. Whether you believe it or not."

Before she could respond, his next patient arrived.

By eight PM, they'd seen every patient, the clinic was empty, and they were both exhausted.

Wesley locked the door behind the last patient and turned to find Sloane sitting on the floor against the wall, shoes kicked off, hair escaping its bun.

"You okay?" he asked.

"I can't feel my feet. Pretty sure I answered the phone forty-seven times. And I think I'm permanently sticky from the humidity." She opened one eye to look at him. "But yeah. I'm okay."

Wesley slid down to sit beside her, close enough their arms touched. "You were amazing today."

"I answered phones and fetched water. Not exactly career achievement."

"You helped twenty people get the care they needed. That's not nothing." He bumped her shoulder gently. "Also, you only complained about my humming twice. Personal record."

She opened both eyes, looking at him. "I'm losing my edge. Soon I'll be making terrible puns."

"Promise?"

"Absolutely not."

"Is this what you meant?" Wesley asked. "About measuring different things?"

Sloane considered the question. "Yeah. This is exactly what I meant."

"How's it feel?"

"Exhausting. Satisfying. Weird." She paused. "Good weird."

"Good weird is my specialty."

They sat in comfortable silence, the clinic cooling finally as the evening temperature dropped outside.

"I'm starting to understand," Sloane said quietly. "Why you stayed. Why you chose this over prestige and credentials."

Wesley turned to look at her. "Yeah?"

"Yeah. And it scares me how much I'm starting to understand it."

"Why does that scare you?"

"Because understanding it means admitting my whole life might have been pointed in the wrong direction." She stared at her hands. "Because if Millbrook Falls feels like home..."

"Then what?"

"Then leaving is going to hurt." The words came out barely above a whisper. "And I don't do hurt well. I do grumpy and defensive and sarcastic. Hurt is too vulnerable."

"You're allowed to be vulnerable sometimes, you know."

"That sounds fake."

"It's real. Promise." Wesley's voice was gentle. "Also, you're terrible at hiding your feelings. Your face does this thing when you're trying not to care."

"What thing?"

"This." He traced a finger between her eyebrows where she always furrowed when anxious. "You get a little wrinkle right here when you're being extra grumpy."

The touch was electric. Sloane's breath caught. "Don't do that."

"Do what? This?" He did it again, slower this time.

"Wesley..."

WESLEY SHIFTED CLOSER until their shoulders were pressed together. "So don't leave."

"It's not that simple—"

"Isn't it? You stay. I'm already here. We see what happens."

"Wesley..."

"Or we don't." His voice dropped lower. "We can keep pretending this thing between us doesn't exist. Keep maintaining professional distance. Keep lying to ourselves. Keep me making terrible puns while you pretend not to be charmed."

"I'm never charmed by your puns."

"Liar. You smiled at the joint effort one. It's my personal favorite."

"That was a grimace."

"It was a smile. I'm an expert on your face now." Wesley turned to face her fully. "I've spent weeks learning exactly what each expression means. I know when you're actually annoyed versus when you're fighting a smile. I know when you're scared versus when you're angry. I know—"

She turned to face him, cutting him off. "What do you want, Wesley?"

His humor faded, replaced by something raw and honest. "I want to kiss you. I've wanted to kiss you since you showed up on Bea's porch with your color-coded charts and determination to control the uncontrollable. Since you called my sourdough metaphor ambitious in that withering tone. Since you rolled your eyes at my very first pun."

Her breath caught. "That's very specific."

"I'm a specific kind of guy." His hand came up to cup her jaw. "With very specific feelings about grumpy consultants who organize my life and accidentally save my patients. So tell me—is this still a terrible idea?"

Sloane leaned into his touch, her eyes fluttering closed. "Absolutely terrible."

"Want to do it anyway?"

"More than I should."

"Is that a yes?"

She opened her eyes, meeting his gaze directly. "Shut up and kiss me."

Wesley grinned. "Yes ma'am."

The first touch of his lips was gentle, questioning. Sloane

answered by fisting her hands in his shirt and pulling him closer.

Wesley made a sound low in his throat and kissed her harder.

His hands came up to frame her face, angling her head to deepen the kiss. Sloane's fingers found their way into his hair, pulling him even closer, trying to eliminate every inch of space between them.

She'd kissed men before. Safe men. Appropriate men. Men who fit into her five-year plan.

But none of them had felt like this—like coming home and jumping off a cliff simultaneously.

Wesley's mouth moved against hers, slow and thorough, like he was in no hurry to discover exactly what made her gasp. One hand slid into her hair, the other settled at her waist, warm and solid.

When they finally broke apart, both breathing hard, Sloane couldn't look away from him.

"We just complicated everything," she whispered.

"I know." Wesley kissed her again, softer this time. "Don't care."

She tasted like summer and home, like everything he'd been trying not to want.

When Sloane made that small sound in the back of her throat—half sigh, half surrender—Wesley was completely, utterly lost.

This was dangerous. Falling for someone who'd been honest that this was never going to be permanent. Who had an interview in Chicago in four days. Who'd made it clear Vermont was temporary.

But with Sloane in his arms, mouth soft and eager against his, danger felt worth it.

Her hands were in his hair, on his shoulders, mapping his

back. Every touch sent fire through his system. He pulled her closer, impossibly closer, until she was practically in his lap.

When they broke apart for air, Wesley rested his forehead against hers.

"That was—" He couldn't finish the sentence.

"Yeah," Sloane agreed breathlessly. "It was."

Her fingers traced patterns on the back of his neck, sending shivers down his spine. Wesley could see gold flecks in her eyes this close, could count the freckles across her nose.

"We should probably talk about this," Sloane said, but she didn't pull away.

"Probably." Wesley kissed her again, quick and sweet. "But right now I really want to kiss you again."

She pulled him back, eliminating the small space between them. "Talk later. Kiss now."

"I love the way you think," Wesley murmured against her mouth.

They kissed until the rain stopped, until the clinic cooled completely, until Sloane's phone buzzed with a text from Bea asking if she'd gotten lost.

They finally pulled apart, laughing breathlessly, when Sloane's phone buzzed for the third time.

"Bea's going to send a search party," Sloane said, not moving from where she'd somehow ended up straddling Wesley's lap.

"Let her." Wesley's hands were warm on her waist, keeping her close. "This is important."

"This is crazy."

"Best kind of crazy."

Sloane traced his jawline with her finger, watching his

eyes darken. "I'm leaving Sunday. For Chicago. That hasn't changed."

"I know."

"I don't know what I want. I don't know if I can—"

"Sloane." Wesley caught her hand, pressed a kiss to her palm. "I'm not asking you to know. I'm just asking you to stop running long enough to see where this could go."

"What if it goes nowhere?"

"Then at least we'll know." He pulled her down for another kiss, soft and lingering. "But what if it goes somewhere amazing?"

Her phone buzzed again.

"Go." Wesley helped her stand, though he kept hold of her hand. "Before Bea actually calls the police."

Sloane grabbed her shoes, her bag, trying to remember how to be a functional human instead of a puddle of desire and confusion.

At the door, she turned back. Wesley was still sitting on the floor, hair mussed from her fingers, lips swollen from kissing, looking at her like she hung the moon.

"Wesley?"

"Yeah?"

"That was—" She couldn't find the words. "I'm not sorry."

His smile could have powered the entire town. "Me neither. Not even a little bit."

"Even though it's complicated?"

"Especially because it's complicated." Wesley stood, crossed to her, kissed her once more. "See you tomorrow for Bea's session?"

"I'll be there."

"Good." He traced her lower lip with his thumb. "Because I have at least seventeen more terrible puns I've been saving up. Also, I want to do this again."

"The puns or the kissing?"

"Both. Definitely both."

Sloane laughed, feeling lighter than she had in months. "You're impossible."

WESLEY LOCKED up the clinic and sat in his truck for a long moment, touching his lips like he could still feel her there.

He'd kissed Sloane Hartwell.

More than that—she'd kissed him back. Had pulled him closer, made those sounds, looked at him like he mattered.

His phone buzzed. Cora: *Tell me everything.*

How do you even know?

Bea texted the whole town that Sloane's been at your clinic for five hours. We've been taking bets on whether you finally grew a spine.

Wesley grinned. *We kissed.*

Three dots. Three dots. Three dots.

Finally: *ABOUT DAMN TIME.*

She's still leaving Sunday.

For now.

For now, Wesley agreed.

Because maybe—just maybe—kissing in a cooling clinic after fixing an air conditioning crisis was the start of something worth staying for.

Or at least worth coming back to.

BEA TOOK one look at Sloane's face and smiled.

"So. The air conditioning emergency."

"Was very emergency-ish." Sloane tried to sound normal. Failed spectacularly.

"Mmm. And you helped Wesley manage it."

"I did. Very professionally."

"I'm sure." Bea's eyes twinkled. "That's why your lips are

swollen and you're glowing like you've been thoroughly kissed."

Sloane touched her mouth self-consciously. "We... talked."

"Is that what we're calling it?"

"We kissed." The words burst out of her. "In his clinic. On the floor. For probably an hour. Maybe more. I lost track of time."

"And?"

"And it was—" Sloane sank onto the sofa. "It was everything I didn't know I wanted. Which is terrifying because I'm still leaving Sunday for Chicago and I still don't know what I want and everything is so complicated. The only plan I have is the one I made before I came here."

"Or," Bea suggested gently, "maybe everything just became very simple."

Sloane's phone buzzed. Text from Wesley: *Still thinking about you. Also, smile number 47 today. New record. You're welcome.*

Despite everything—the confusion, the fear, the Chicago interview looming—Sloane smiled.

Number 48.

CHAPTER 8

Sloane woke up smiling.

For exactly three seconds, she floated in that perfect space between sleep and consciousness where everything felt right with the world.

Then reality crashed in.

What did I do? What did we do?

She'd kissed Wesley Nakamura. In his clinic. On the floor. Multiple times. Extensively.

And now everything was different.

Sloane grabbed her phone, checking the time. 6:47 AM. She had emails to answer, job applications to update—because the one in Chicago wasn't guaranteed—a life plan to follow. Wesley Nakamura and his patient eyes and his gentle hands and the way he'd glanced at her when no one was looking. Like she was the only thing that mattered—that was NOT part of the plan.

But she couldn't stop smiling when she thought about it.

Her phone buzzed. Text from Wesley: *Morning. Can't stop thinking about last night. Coffee before Bea's session?*

Sloane stared at the screen.

This was real. She'd kissed him and he'd kissed her back and now everything was different and complicated and terrifying and—

She was still smiling.

Coffee sounds good, she typed back. *Why don't I come to the clinic. Bea needs her rest.*

Actually she wanted to see him without Bea's peanut gallery comments.

Perfect. I'll bring the good stuff from the bakery. Also, I've been working on a new pun. It's terrible. You'll hate it. Can't wait to see your face when you hear it.

Despite everything, Sloane laughed.

You're impossible.

You're grumpy. See you at 8:30.

Wesley had been at the clinic since 7 AM, trying to work and failing miserably.

He'd kissed Sloane Hartwell last night. Multiple times. Extensively. And it had been even better than the weeks of anticipation had suggested.

Now he was nervous, which was new.

He'd kissed plenty of people. But none of them had been Sloane—complicated, ambitious, temporary Sloane who'd crashed into his life and made him want things he'd given up on.

What if she regretted it? What if the light of day brought back all her corporate rationality and professional boundaries? What if she'd decided last night was a mistake?

The sound of her BMW pulling into the parking lot made his heart rate spike.

Get it together, Wesley told himself. *You're a grown man. You can handle a conversation about feelings.*

Sloane walked in carrying her tablet and wearing her

professional armor—pressed blouse, tailored pants, hair perfectly styled. But when their eyes met, she smiled, and something in Wesley's chest loosened.

"Hi," she said.

"Hi." Wesley couldn't stop looking at her. "You came."

"You brought coffee. Of course I came."

"I also brought cinnamon rolls."

"Bribery. Smart." But she was moving closer, setting down her tablet.

Wesley searched her face. "Tell me you don't regret it."

Sloane bit her lower lip. "I don't. I should, but I don't."

"Why should you?"

"Because it's complicated. Because I'm leaving. Because you deserve—" She stopped herself.

"I deserve what?"

"More than temporary."

WESLEY TOOK HER HAND, pulling her closer until they were standing right in front of each other.

"How about we let me decide what I deserve? And you decide what you want?"

Sloane looked at their linked hands, then up at his face. "We should probably establish some parameters."

Wesley's lips twitched. "Parameters? For what, exactly?"

She felt heat rise in her face. "For whatever this is. I mean, I'm still job hunting. Still planning to leave eventually. Maybe soon. And you're—"

"I'm what?"

"You're someone who could get hurt. Because I don't know what I want or where I'm going or how any of this is supposed to work."

Wesley tugged her closer until they were nearly chest to chest. "So we figure it out as we go."

"That's not a plan."

"No. It's better than a plan." His thumb traced circles on her palm. "It's honest."

Sloane took a breath. "I want to keep kissing you. But I don't want to hurt you."

"I'm a grown man, Sloane. I can handle my own heart." Wesley squeezed her hand. "The question is—can you handle yours?"

The words hit her like a punch. Could she? Could she let herself feel something real for someone when the future was so uncertain?

"I don't know," she admitted. "But I want to try."

"Then that's enough." Wesley pulled her into a hug, and Sloane let herself sink into it. "We'll take it one day at a time. No promises about the future. Just honest about the present."

"What is the present?"

"The present is—" Wesley pulled back enough to look at her. "—I really want to kiss you good morning."

"That seems unprofessional."

"Definitely unprofessional." But he was already leaning in.

"We're at your place of business."

"Technically we're here thirty minutes before business hours."

"That's a technicality."

"I'm very good with technicalities." Wesley's lips were inches from hers. "Any other objections?"

"Several. But I can't remember them right now."

"Good." He closed the distance.

The kiss was soft, sweet, morning-gentle. Nothing like the desperate passion of last night, but somehow even more intimate for its tenderness.

When they broke apart, Wesley was grinning. "So. Parameters. What did we decide?"

Sloane tried to remember how to think. "No hiding it. Small towns figure things out anyway."

"Agreed. What else?"

"No promises about the future. I'm still figuring things out."

"But honest about the present," Wesley added. "Which is that we want each other."

"Yes." Sloane took a breath. "Is that enough?"

"For now? It's everything."

AT BEA'S morning therapy session, Sloane and Wesley couldn't hide their new intimacy.

They moved around each other differently now. Wesley's hand on her lower back as they passed in the doorway. Sloane's fingers brushing his when she handed him the resistance bands. Shared smiles over Bea's head.

"Well, well," Bea murmured, watching them with undisguised delight. "Something's different this morning."

"Different how?" Sloane tried for innocent.

"You're both glowing. And you keep touching each other like you can't help it." Bea's smile was triumphant. "About time."

Wesley laughed. "That obvious?"

"Darling, you're both terrible at hiding anything. Sloane's been walking around with her head in the clouds all morning, and you keep looking at her like she's the sun and you're a very happy sunflower."

"I don't—" Sloane started.

"You absolutely do," Bea interrupted. "And it's wonderful. Young love should be obvious and joyful and slightly ridiculous."

"It's not love," Sloane protested automatically.

Wesley's hand found hers. "Not yet. But it could be."

The words hung in the air between them—promise and possibility and terrifying potential.

"You two should coordinate more wellness fair activities," Bea suggested with theatrical innocence. "I'm sure you'll work very well together. Closely. For extended periods."

"Aunt Bea—"

"Just making suggestions, darling."

BY NOON, apparently the entire town knew.

Wesley's phone: *FINALLY. Details immediately.* - Cora

Sloane's phone: *Heard you're dating the cute PT. Coffee this week?* - Jackie (who Sloane had only met once at the diner)

At the hardware store picking up supplies for the fair, Margot actually winked at them.

"Young love," she said dreamily. "So beautiful."

"We're not—" Sloane started.

"Oh honey, everyone knows. Mrs. Adams saw you two leaving the clinic together this morning looking very cozy. And Cora mentioned Wesley's been smiling nonstop since yesterday." Margot handed Wesley his paint supplies. "The betting pool paid out, by the way. I won fifty dollars."

Wesley groaned. "There was actual money on this?"

"Of course! Small towns need entertainment." Margot winked again. "Enjoy the honeymoon phase, you two. It's the best part."

Outside, Sloane looked at Wesley in horror. "Everyone knows."

"Small town." Wesley didn't look bothered. "We agreed not to hide it, remember?"

"I didn't think not hiding it meant announcing it via small-town telegraph."

"Same thing here." Wesley caught her hand, lacing their fingers together. "Does it bother you? People knowing?"

Sloane considered. Did it? Being publicly connected to Wesley Nakamura, sunshine physical therapist who made terrible puns and cared too much and kissed like he had something to prove?

"No," she realized. "It doesn't bother me."

Wesley's smile could have powered the entire state. "Good. Because Cordelia's headed this way and she definitely wants to give us relationship advice."

"Oh god."

"Too late to run."

"Wesley! Sloane!" Cordelia materialized like she'd been waiting for this exact moment. "I heard the wonderful news."

"News travels fast," Sloane said weakly.

"Of course it does, dear. This is Millbrook Falls. We have three channels of entertainment: the waterfall, the weather, and each other's business." Cordelia beamed at them both. "Summer romances are my favorite. There's something about the heat that makes people finally admit what they've been feeling."

"Mrs. Ashworth—" Wesley started.

"Now, I'm not saying you should rush into anything. But I am saying that when you know, you know." Cordelia's eyes twinkled. "My late husband proposed after three weeks. Everyone said we were crazy. We had forty-seven wonderful years together."

"We're not—" Sloane began.

"Not ready to think about that yet. Of course not. I'm just saying—" Cordelia patted Sloane's hand "—don't let fear of the unknown keep you from experiencing something beautiful. Sometimes the best things in life don't come with guarantees."

After Cordelia left, Sloane and Wesley stood in silence.

"She's right, you know," Wesley said quietly.

"About what?"

"The best things don't come with guarantees." He looked at her. "But they're still worth it."

THAT EVENING, Wesley was doing paperwork when his phone rang. Unknown number.

He almost didn't answer.

"Hello?"

"Wesley. It's Devon."

The voice hit him like cold water. Devon. His ex. The woman who'd left him behind two years ago without looking back.

"Devon. I'm surprised to hear from you."

"I know, right? It's been forever." Devon's voice was warm, familiar, painful. "I'm in Vermont for work. Thought we could catch up?"

Wesley's stomach dropped. "You're here? In Vermont?"

"Burlington. Client meeting. But I'm free tomorrow night. We could grab dinner? For old times' sake?"

Old times. When Wesley had believed Devon might stay. When he'd thought love could overcome geography and ambition and fundamental incompatibility.

"I don't think that's a good idea."

"Come on, Wesley. We're adults. Surely you're over the breakup by now? I've missed you."

Devon who'd left him behind without looking back. Devon who represented everything he'd thought he wanted —ambition, success, escape from small-town limitations.

But now all he could think about was Sloane. Complicated, temporary Sloane who made him laugh and challenged him and kissed him like he mattered.

"I'm seeing someone."

Devon laughed. "In Millbrook Falls? Come on. How serious could it be?"

The words hit his insecurity dead center. Sloane was temporary. Was leaving for Chicago Sunday for an interview. Had made no promises about the future.

How serious *could* it be?

"It's serious," Wesley said, more firmly than he felt.

"If you say so. But the offer stands. I'm here until Friday. Would be good to see you." Devon's voice softened. "I was wrong, Wesley. About a lot of things. I just want a chance to say that in person."

After hanging up, Wesley sat staring at nothing.

Devon was here. In Vermont. Wanting to see him.

Devon who'd broken his heart.

Devon who'd made him swear off temporary people.

Devon who was now a ghost from a past he'd thought he was over.

He should tell Sloane. Should mention it. Should be transparent about the fact that his ex had just called wanting to have dinner.

But she was already scared. Already planning her exit. Already convinced this couldn't last.

Telling her about Devon would just add pressure she didn't need.

I'll handle it myself, Wesley decided. *No need to worry her about ghosts from my past.*

It was a mistake.

He knew it was a mistake even as he made the decision.

THAT EVENING, Wesley picked Sloane up for a walk around the falls.

Something was off. He was distracted, quieter than usual. When she asked if he was okay, he smiled and said he was fine.

But Sloane had spent eight years reading people in corporate settings where tiny differences could signal big changes. Although she'd missed the downsizing thing. Wesley was *not* fine.

"You sure?" she pressed.

"Just a long day." He took her hand. "Too many patients, not enough air conditioning."

It wasn't the whole truth. Sloane could tell. But she didn't push.

Maybe he needed space. Maybe she was overthinking. Maybe new relationships were just awkward and uncertain and she needed to relax.

They walked in comfortable silence, watching the waterfall catch the sunset. Wesley's thumb traced patterns on her palm. When they stopped at the overlook, he pulled her close, kissing her temple.

"This is nice," he said.

"Yeah. It is."

"I'm glad you're here."

"Me too." And she meant it.

When he walked her back to Bea's cottage, Wesley kissed her goodnight—soft, sweet, reassuring.

"See you tomorrow?"

"Tomorrow," Sloane agreed.

But as she watched him drive away, doubt crept in. Something had changed. Something he wasn't telling her.

Stop it, she told herself. *Not everything is a crisis. Sometimes people are just tired.*

Inside, Bea was waiting with a small glass of whiskey.

"How was your walk?"

"Good. Wesley was a bit quiet."

"Hmm. That's not like him."

"I know." Sloane wrapped her hands around her mug. "Maybe he's having second thoughts. About us. About dating someone who's temporary."

"Or," Bea suggested, "maybe he's just processing. New relationships are complicated, darling. Give him time."

"I don't have time. I leave for Chicago Sunday."

"Then make the most of the time you have." Bea sipped her tea. "And stop borrowing trouble. If something's wrong, he'll tell you."

But as Sloane lay in bed that night, she couldn't shake the feeling that something had shifted.

And neither of them had been honest about it.

WESLEY STARED AT HIS PHONE, Devon's contact information still on the screen. He should delete it. Should block the number. Should tell Sloane about the call.

Instead, he typed to Cora: *Devon called. She's in Vermont. Wants to meet up.*

Three dots. Then: *What did you say?*

That I'm seeing someone.

Did you tell Sloane?

Wesley stared at the question. *Not yet.*

Wesley.

I know. I will. I just... I don't want to worry her about something that doesn't matter.

It matters if it's affecting you. And it clearly is.

I'm fine.

You're lying. To me and to yourself.

Wesley tossed his phone aside, running his hands through his hair.

He was fine. Devon was the past. Sloane was the present. There was nothing to tell because nothing was going to happen.

CHAPTER 9

"This is ridiculous," Sloane said as Wesley helped her into a kayak. "I have emails to answer. Application materials to update."

"You have plenty of time for all that." Wesley settled into his own kayak with practiced ease. "And you've been staring at your laptop since 6 AM. You need a break."

"I don't need—"

"Sloane. Get in the kayak. Trust me."

She got in the kayak.

Twenty minutes later, floating on the lake with mountains reflected in glass-still water, Sloane felt something loosen in her chest.

No laptop. No phone signal. No job rejection emails waiting to ruin her morning. Just sunshine and birdsong and the gentle lap of water against her kayak.

"This is nice," she admitted quietly.

Wesley paddled closer, grinning triumphantly. "That didn't kill you, did it? Just existing?"

"Don't get cocky." She splashed him with her paddle.

"Too late. Already composing victory speech." He guided

his kayak right up next to hers. "You're beautiful out here, you know. Without the armor. Just you and the sunshine."

"That's sappy."

"It's true." Wesley leaned across the small space between their kayaks and kissed her.

Sweet at first, then deeper. His hand caressed her cheek, angling her head for better access. Sloane's fingers gripped the edge of his kayak for balance as the kiss intensified.

When they broke apart, both breathing hard, their kayaks had drifted together and were now bumping companionably against each other.

"Making out in kayaks is complicated," Sloane observed.

"Very complicated." Wesley was still close enough to kiss again. "Worth it though."

"Definitely worth it."

They floated like that for another hour, talking about nothing and everything. Sloane laughed more than she had in months. And when Wesley finally paddled them back to shore, she realized she'd completely forgotten about her interview prep.

For the first time in eight years, work hadn't been her first priority.

It was terrifying and wonderful in equal measure.

TWO DAYS LATER, Sloane showed up at the clinic with her tablet and a determined expression.

"We're implementing systems," she announced. "I can't just keep moving files around hoping a sense of order will suddenly appear."

Wesley looked up from his paperwork. "We are?"

"Your filing system is stretching the definition of system. "She was already moving toward the disaster zone. "We're fixing it."

"I like my system—"

"You don't have a system." But she was smiling. "Let me help. Please. I need to feel useful and this is what I'm good at."

Wesley watched her work for the next two hours. The way she saw patterns, created order from chaos—it was like watching an artist. Or maybe he was completely hopeless at organization and this was just basics. It didn't matter, she was here and not leaving. He'd take what he could get.

She was in her element, explaining efficiency with her whole body—gesturing, demonstrating, completely animated. "If you move the supply closet here and add these labels—"

Wesley couldn't help himself. He pulled her into his arms.

"What are you doing?" But she was laughing.

"You're beautiful when you're organizing."

"That's a weird compliment."

"You light up when you solve problems." He kissed her neck. "It's sexy."

"Sexy? I'm literally alphabetizing records."

"Incredibly sexy." Wesley turned her to face him properly. "I love watching your mind work."

The kiss started sweet but quickly deepened. Sloane's back hit the filing cabinet with a soft thud, Wesley's body pressing against hers. Her hands fisted in his shirt, pulling him closer.

This was different from the kayak kissing. Hungrier. More urgent. His hands slid under her shirt, finding bare skin, and Sloane made a sound that went straight through him.

They heard footsteps in the hallway.

Both jumped apart, breathing hard, just as Cora walked in with patient files.

"Oh. Hi." Cora looked between them, taking in their flushed faces and disheveled appearance. "I'm interrupting."

"No," Sloane said too quickly. "We were just—"

"Organizing," Wesley finished lamely.

Cora's smile was knowing. "Uh-huh. Well, when you're done organizing, Mrs. Patterson is here for her 2 PM."

After Cora left, Sloane and Wesley looked at each other and burst out laughing.

"We're terrible at this," Sloane said.

"Terrible at what? Maintaining professional boundaries?"

"That. Also, lying." She was still pressed against the filing cabinet, Wesley's hands still on her hips. "We should probably stop making out in your clinic."

"Probably." But Wesley kissed her again, anyway. "Starting tomorrow."

"Starting tomorrow," she agreed.

THAT FRIDAY, Wesley invited Sloane to dinner at his apartment.

Sloane stood outside his door, nervous in a way she hadn't been since their first kiss. This felt like an escalation. Going to his place. Alone. After the near-miss making out session at the clinic.

She knocked before she could overthink it.

Wesley opened the door, and Sloane forgot why she'd been nervous. He was in jeans and a t-shirt, barefoot, relaxed in a way she'd never seen him at work. His apartment was warm and lived-in—bookshelves overflowing, plants in every window, artwork covering the walls.

"This is very you," she said, looking around.

"Is that good or bad?"

"Good. Very good." She turned to face him. "It's perfect."

The dinner was simple—pasta, salad, wine. But Wesley

cooked competently, moving around his small kitchen with easy confidence. They talked while he worked—about his family, her childhood, the jobs they'd loved and hated, dreams they'd given up on and ones they hadn't.

Hours passed without notice.

They moved to the couch with their wine. The conversation turned more intimate—past relationships, current fears, what they wanted from life.

"I thought I wanted the corporate track," Sloane admitted. "Credentials, prestige, six-figure salary. But I was miserable."

"What do you want now?"

"I don't know. That's what scares me." She looked at him. "I'm starting to think maybe I want something different. Something slower. Something more... real."

Wesley set down his wine glass. "Something like this?"

"Maybe. Possibly. I don't know." But she was leaning closer. "Is that okay? Not knowing?"

"It's honest." Wesley closed the remaining distance. "That's better than okay."

The kiss started slow but quickly intensified. Wesley pulled Sloane into his lap, her legs straddling his thighs. His hands slid under her shirt, warm against her skin. Sloane's fingers tangled in his hair as the kiss deepened.

They were horizontal on the couch now, Wesley's weight pressing her into the cushions. His mouth moved from her lips to her jaw to her neck, and Sloane's breath came in gasps.

"Wesley—"

He lifted his head, looking at her with dark eyes. "Yeah?"

"I want—" She couldn't finish the sentence.

Wesley pressed his forehead against hers, breathing hard. "I want you too. But only if you're sure."

Sloane's hands were shaking. "I want you. But I'm scared."

"Of what?"

"Of this meaning too much. Of hurting you when I leave. Of—" Her voice broke. "Of wanting to stay so much that I give up everything I worked for."

Wesley rolled to his side, pulling her against his chest. "Then we wait. No pressure. We have time."

"Do we?" Sloane whispered. "The interview is Sunday. If they offer me a position—"

"Then we'll figure it out." Wesley's arms tightened around her. "But right now, we're here. That's enough."

They lay like that for a long time, tangled together, not talking. Eventually, Sloane's breathing evened out, and Wesley realized she'd fallen asleep.

He covered them both with a blanket and let himself just hold her.

For tonight, this was enough.

SATURDAY MORNING, Wesley stopped at the coffee shop for his usual order. Sloane was in deep preparation for her interview and he felt like he was walking with a hole at his side. How could he miss her so much this soon?

He turned to leave and walked directly into Devon Cross.

Devon looked exactly the same—expensive suit, perfect hair, everything Wesley had once thought he wanted. Sophisticated, successful, representing every ambition Wesley had given up. Until Sloane.

"Wesley." Devon's smile was warm, familiar. "You look good. Small-town life agrees with you."

The condescension was subtle but there. Wesley heard it loud and clear.

"Devon. I thought you were in Burlington."

"Client meeting ran late. Thought I'd get reacquainted with Millbrook Falls before heading back to Boston." Devon gestured around the small coffee shop with barely concealed amusement. "Nothing's changed, I see."

"What do you want, Devon?"

"To talk. To apologize properly." Devon stepped closer. "Can we sit?"

Wesley should say no. Should walk away. Should maintain the boundaries he'd spent two years building.

Instead, he sat. Trying to ignore the feeling he was cheating on Sloane.

"Still playing with geriatric patients?" Devon asked, sipping her latte. "I'm at Mass General now. Sports medicine department. Finally doing the work we talked about. The work you wanted to do."

Twist of old pain, sharp and unexpected. "Good for you."

"It could have been us. Both of us. If you'd come to Boston like I asked." Devon leaned forward. "I made a mistake leaving, Wesley. I've thought about you every day for two years. Give me another chance."

Wesley's world tilted. "You're not serious."

"Completely serious. We were good together. We could be again."

"I'm with someone."

Devon glanced around the coffee shop. "The one you mentioned? Seriously? What does she do, run the general store?"

Wesley bristled. "She's a consultant. And it's none of your business."

"Is she from here?" Devon's tone was sharp now. "Or is she another city person slumming in Vermont before going back to her real life?"

Direct hit. Wesley felt it land like a physical blow.

"She's—" He stopped. Because he couldn't answer. Because it was true. Sloane was temporary. Was leaving. Had an interview in Chicago tomorrow.

Devon saw his hesitation and smiled. "That's what I thought. History repeating itself, isn't it? You fall for ambition and then act surprised when it leaves."

"This is different—"

"Is it? Because from here, it looks exactly the same." Devon stood. "Think about it. I'm offering you everything you gave up—career, prestige, the chance to work at an elite hospital. And I'm offering myself. Someone who actually understands your potential instead of keeping you buried in this dead-end town."

After Devon left, Wesley sat in the coffee shop, staring at nothing.

Devon was wrong about Millbrook Falls. Wrong about Wesley's choices. Wrong about everything that mattered.

But she was right about one thing: Sloane was exactly like Devon. Brilliant, ambitious, using small-town Vermont as a way station between her real life.

And Wesley was falling in love with her, anyway.

THAT AFTERNOON, Cora invited Sloane for coffee.

"So, you and Wesley," Cora said, grinning. "The whole town is talking."

Sloane had no time for this. She'd agreed to meet Cora because Bea said she should take a break from her presentations. "Of course they are."

"It's adorable. He's been alone since his ex left two years ago. Everyone's happy he's finally moving on. Of course he as talking to her this morning."

Sloane's stomach dropped. "His ex?"

"Devon Cross. Total catch—successful, gorgeous, apparently wanting Wesley back." Cora sipped her coffee, oblivious to Sloane's reaction. "Saw her in town yesterday."

The words hit like a punch.

"Sloane? You okay?"

"I'm fine." But she wasn't. "Cora, was Wesley... was he serious about Devon?"

"Very serious. Everyone thought they'd get married. Then Devon got a job offer in Boston and left without looking back. Wesley was devastated for months."

After Cora left, Sloane sat alone with her coffee and her thoughts. First, why had she brought up this Devon? She'd thought Cora was on her side, but it felt like a warning.

Maybe it was, she was exactly like the person who hurt him. Exactly like Devon. Ambitious, planning her exit. Ignoring the feelings that told her to stay.

The Chicago interview was Monday. If they offered her the position, she'd take it. She had to. It was everything she'd been working toward. But the thought of leaving Wesley—of being another person who chose ambition over him—made her chest ache.

She'd been so focused on her own fear of staying, she hadn't considered that Wesley was terrified of being left again.

And she was going to leave. Eventually. Probably.

Wasn't she?

LATER, Wesley picked Sloane up for their usual walk.

He was distant. Quiet. When she tried to take his hand, his fingers were stiff.

"Something's wrong," Sloane said finally. "Did I do something?"

"No. Just tired."

"Don't do that. Don't shut me out."

Wesley stopped walking, turning to face her. "You want honesty? Fine. My ex is in town asking for another chance."

Sloane's world tilted.

Wesley squeezed her hand. "You knew. About Devon?"

"Cora mentioned—" She stopped. "You didn't tell me."

"I was going to—"

"When? After she left? After you decided whether you wanted her back?"

"It's not like that—" Wesley ran his hands through his hair, frustration clear on his face. "You want to know what Devon said? She said I have a pattern. Falling for ambitious people who use Millbrook Falls as a rest stop before their real life."

Sloane flinched. "Wesley—"

"And I can't help thinking about how you're exactly like her. Brilliant, ambitious, counting down days until you leave." His voice broke. "I knew this. I knew you were temporary. But I fell for you anyway like an idiot."

"That's not fair—"

"Isn't it? Can you honestly tell me you don't have one foot out the door? That you're not planning your exit even while you're kissing me?"

Silence. She couldn't lie.

Wesley's laugh was bitter. "That's what I thought."

"You know I'm leaving tomorrow for an interview on Monday. I never kept that a secret," Sloane said quietly. "In Chicago. Morrison & Associates. If they offer me a position—"

"You'll take it."

"I don't know—"

"Yes, you do. Because it's everything you want. Career, prestige, escape from dead-end Vermont and the small-town physical therapist who was stupid enough to fall for you. Bea's doing fine, she doesn't need you here."

"That's not—" But Sloane's voice broke. "I don't know what I want. That's the problem. I don't know if I want Chicago or if I want—"

"Me?" Wesley's eyes were dark with pain. "You can't even say it."

"Because I'm scared! Because wanting you means giving up everything I thought I was supposed to be. Because choosing you means admitting my entire life plan was wrong." Tears were streaming down her face now. "And I don't know if I'm brave enough to do that."

Wesley turned and walked away, leaving Sloane standing alone in the fading light.

WESLEY SAT in his dark apartment, phone in his hand.

He'd been a fool. Fallen for exactly the wrong person again. At least Devon had been honest about her ambitions from the start. Sloane kept talking like maybe she'd stay while building her exit strategy.

His phone buzzed. Text from Cora: *Heard about the fight. You okay?*

No.

Want to talk?

No.

Going to hide and brood instead?

That's the plan.

But his apartment felt empty. His days felt longer. Everything reminded him of her—the organized everything in sight, the way she took her coffee, the sound of her laugh when he made terrible puns.

He'd fallen in love with Sloane Hartwell.

And she was leaving anyway.

SLOANE SOBBED the moment she stepped inside.

Bea took one look at her and pulled her into a hug.

"I'm doing exactly what his ex did," Sloane sobbed. "Leading him on when I know I'm going to leave."

"Do you know that?" Bea's voice was gentle. "Or are you so scared of wanting to stay that you're forcing yourself to leave?"

"I don't know. I don't know what I want anymore."

"Then maybe it's time to figure it out." Bea pulled back, looking at Sloane directly. "Before you lose something you can't get back."

"But what if I stay and it doesn't work? What if I give up my career and in two years we break up anyway and I have nothing?"

"And what if you leave and spend the rest of your life wondering what might have been?" Bea's eyes were kind but firm. "What if you get your dream job and realize it wasn't the dream you wanted anymore?"

Sloane curled up on the sofa, Bea's words echoing in her head.

The Chicago interview was only one day away. It didn't feel like enough time to decide if she wanted the life she'd planned or the life she'd accidentally found.

Her phone buzzed. Text from the wellness fair committee: *Fair meeting Friday. Need both coordinators present.*

She and Wesley would have to work together. Would have to be professional. Would have to pretend they weren't both miserable. And by Friday she would know if she was moving to Chicago.

Sloane stared at the ceiling, tears still streaming down her face.

She'd fallen in love with Wesley Nakamura.

And she had no idea what to do about it.

CHAPTER 10

The flight was turbulent. Sloane took it as an omen.

Chicago was exactly what she remembered from her early corporate days—glass towers, power suits, everyone moving with purpose and urgency. Her hotel was sleek and modern and utterly devoid of personality.

She ordered room service, reviewed her presentation materials, and absolutely did not think about Wesley.

Except she did. Constantly.

Wondered what he was doing. Whether he missed her. Whether he'd already moved on, decided she wasn't worth the trouble of someone complicated and temporary.

Her phone buzzed. Text from Cora: *Good luck with your interview! Wesley's been moping around town like a sad puppy. Just FYI.*

Sloane stared at the message.

He was moping?

She wanted to text him. Or call to hear his voice, even if they were fighting. But she didn't know what to say.

I'm in Chicago preparing to interview for a job I'm not

sure I want anymore but I'm too scared to admit that out loud.

Yeah. That would go over great.

Sloane turned off her phone and tried to sleep.

WESLEY WAS SKIMMING professional articles without retaining any information when someone knocked on the clinic door.

He wasn't open on Sundays. Whoever it was could come back tomorrow.

The knocking continued.

"Wesley, I know you're in there. Your truck is outside."

He froze.

That voice. He knew that voice.

Devon Cross stood on his doorstep in designer jeans and a silk blouse. She should have left him.

"What do you want, Devon?"

"To talk. Please." Her smile was the one that used to make his heart race. Now it just made him tired. "Can I come in?"

Against his better judgment, Wesley let her in.

Devon looked around the clinic, her expression carefully neutral. "It's... nice. Cozy."

"It's a small-town practice. Not exactly Mass General."

"I wasn't criticizing." Devon turned to face him. "I've been thinking about what I said at the coffee shop. I was out of line. Condescending."

"Yeah. You were."

"I'm sorry." Devon stepped closer. "I was defensive because seeing you again made me realize what I gave up. You look happy here, Wesley. Content. Like you found exactly where you belong."

"I did."

"With her? The consultant?"

Wesley's jaw tightened. "That's none of your business."

"Except she's not here, is she?" Devon's voice was gentle, knowing. "I asked around town. Everyone says she left for Chicago. For a job interview."

"So?"

"Another ambitious woman choosing career over you, over this place." Devon reached for his hand. "I know how that feels, Wesley. I did the same thing to you. And I told you I've regretted it every single day."

Wesley pulled his hand away. "What are you saying?"

"I'm saying I made a mistake. Mass General is prestigious, but it's lonely. Boston is expensive and cold and I haven't met anyone who makes me laugh like you did. Who sees me the way you did." Devon's eyes were earnest, almost desperate. "Give me another chance. Let me prove I can choose you this time."

Wesley stared at her. He'd already said no. Why couldn't she hear that? Even if Sloane moved to Chicago, he didn't want Devon back.

Two years ago, this would have been everything he wanted. Devon admitting she was wrong, offering him the second chance he'd dreamed about. He was glad Devon didn't offer that chance. He wouldn't be free.

Now all he wanted was Sloane.

Sloane who challenged him and called his puns terrible and organized his chaos with fierce competence. Sloane who was scared and prickly and beautiful when she smiled. Sloane who was in Chicago right now, probably acing her interview, preparing to build the life she deserved.

Sloane who he'd pushed away because he was too scared to fight for her.

"I can't," Wesley said quietly.

"Why not? Because of her? Wesley, she's going to leave just like I did—"

"Maybe she will. Maybe she won't. But Devon, the reason I can't give you another chance isn't because of Sloane." He looked at her directly. "It's because I don't love you anymore. And I'm not sure I ever loved you the way I should have."

Devon flinched. "What does that mean?"

"It means I loved the idea of you. The ambition, the success, the escape from small-town limitations. But you never loved this life and you made it clear you couldn't love me without trying to change me."

"That's not true—"

"It is true. You wanted me to be someone else. Someone successful by your standards. And I tried, Devon. I really tried. But I was miserable." Wesley clenched his hands in frustration that Devon didn't get it. "Sloane sees me exactly as I am—small-town physical therapist who makes ridiculous puns and drives a beat-up Subaru—and she doesn't want to change any of it."

"Until she leaves for her real career."

"Maybe. But at least she's honest about who she is and what she's afraid of. And that's more than you ever gave me."

Devon was silent for a long moment. "You're in love with her."

"Yeah. I am."

"Does she know?"

Wesley laughed bitterly. "I'm not going to stop her leaving. I don't know if she believes I love her. Because I won't leave here either."

"Wesley—"

"You should go, Devon. Go back to Boston, back to Mass General, back to the life you chose. I hope you find someone who makes you happy. But it's not going to be me."

After Devon left, Wesley sat in his empty clinic and finally let himself cry.

Not for Devon. For Sloane.

For the chance he'd thrown away because he was afraid to trust that someone might actually choose him.

THE MORRISON & Associates offices occupied three floors of a glass tower overlooking Lake Michigan.

Sloane wore her best suit, her most professional demeanor, and absolutely none of her heart.

The interview was a blur. Senior partners asking about her experience. Case studies to analyze. A presentation on strategic planning she'd prepared meticulously.

She performed perfectly.

Hit every answer, impressed everyone in the room, demonstrated exactly why she was qualified for the senior consultant position.

And felt absolutely nothing.

"Ms. Hartwell, that was excellent," Jennifer Chen said after the presentation. "Truly exceptional. We'd like to move forward with an offer."

Sloane's heart should have been racing. This was it. Everything she'd been working toward.

"Thank you. I'm very interested in the position."

"We'll have the formal offer letter to you by Wednesday. But I can tell you now—the compensation package is very competitive. Six figures, full benefits, partnership track within three years."

Partnership track. Everything she'd dreamed about.

"That's wonderful. I look forward to reviewing the details."

Professional. Polished. Perfectly corporate.

Completely empty inside.

. . .

After the interview, Sloane had three hours before her flight back to Vermont.

She walked along the lake front, watching Chicago bustle around her. This could be her life—downtown apartment, corporate power, prestigious firm. Everything she'd lost when she got laid off, she could have again.

Her phone rang. Bea.

"How did it go, darling?"

"I got the offer. They're sending formal paperwork Wednesday."

"Congratulations." Bea's voice was carefully neutral. "That's wonderful news."

"Is it?"

"You tell me."

Sloane sat on a bench overlooking the water. "I performed perfectly. Said all the right things. Impressed all the right people. And I felt nothing, Aunt Bea. Nothing. No excitement, no pride, no sense of accomplishment. Just... emptiness."

"That's a lot of what you didn't feel. What did you feel?"

"Like I was playing a part. Like I was pretending to be someone I used to be but don't fit into anymore." Sloane watched sailboats on the water. "In Millbrook Falls, I feel things. I get frustrated and challenged and genuinely happy. Here, I just feel competent."

"Competent is important, darling. But it's not everything."

"I know." Sloane checked her watch. "I need to head to the airport. I'll be home by eight."

"Home."

Sloane ended the call and stared at her phone.

Home.

When had Millbrook Falls become home?

When had a small Vermont town and a sunny physical

therapist become more important than everything she'd worked for?

And what was she going to do about it?

WESLEY'S PHONE interrupted Mrs. Patterson's session.

Text from Bea: *Sloane's flight lands at 8 PM. She got the job offer. Thought you should know.*

Wesley's heart sank.

Of course she got the offer. She was brilliant and capable and exactly what any firm would want.

"Wesley, dear, you're distracted," Mrs. Patterson observed.

"Sorry. Just got some news."

"About Sloane?"

Was there anyone in this town who didn't know their business?

"She got a job offer. Chicago."

Mrs. Patterson made a disapproving sound. "And you're just going to let her take it?"

"What am I supposed to do? Show up at the airport with flowers and beg her to stay?"

"Yes! That's exactly what you're supposed to do." Mrs. Patterson sat up straighter despite her hip pain. "Wesley Nakamura, you're an intelligent man, but you're being remarkably stupid about this. That girl loves you. Everyone can see it except apparently you two."

"She's taking the job—"

"She hasn't taken anything yet. She just got the offer today. Which means she hasn't decided. Which means there's still time to fight for her."

Wesley stared at his patient. "You think I should go to the airport?"

"I think you should stop being a coward and tell her how you feel. Before it's too late."

. . .

SLOANE'S PLANE landed at 6:52 PM.

She walked through the small Vermont airport in a daze, pulling her carry-on behind her. Getting her car and driving to Bea's felt like it took seconds, and years.

Bea was waiting in the living room on the couch. Her can beside her even though Wesley told her to use the walker.

"How are you feeling?" Sloane asked, hugging her aunt.

"Better than you, apparently. You look exhausted."

"It's been a long day."

"Are you going to take the job?"

"I don't know." Sloane stared out the window at mountains silhouetted against the darkening sky. "They're sending the formal offer Wednesday. I have to respond by Friday."

"That's not much time."

"No."

"Have you talked to Wesley?"

"No." Sloane's chest ached. "He'll tell me to take the job. To build the life I'm supposed to have."

"Did you ask if that's what he really wants?"

The question stopped her. "No."

"Why not?"

"Because—" Sloane struggled for words. "Because I shouldn't have to ask. Because if he wanted me to stay, he should have said so. Because I'm terrified of choosing him and having it not be enough."

WESLEY SAT in his apartment at midnight, phone in his hand. He'd drafted and deleted seventeen texts to Sloane.

Congratulations on the job offer. Too formal.

I miss you. Too vulnerable.

Please don't go. Too desperate.

Finally, he just typed: *Can we talk?* His finger hovered over send. But before he could press it, his phone rang.

Cora. "Tell me you did something brave today," she said without preamble.

"Devon came by."

"And?"

"I told her I'm in love with Sloane. That I don't love her anymore and never really did."

"Well, that's something. Did you tell Sloane you love her?"

"No."

"Wesley—"

"She got the job offer, Cora. Chicago. Everything she wanted."

"So fight for her! Go to her. Tell her how you feel. Give her a reason to stay!"

"I can't be the reason she gives up her dreams—"

"Stop hiding behind nobility." Cora's voice was sharp. "You're scared. That's fine. But don't pretend you're protecting her when you're really protecting yourself."

After hanging up, Wesley looked at his unsent text. *Can we talk?* He deleted it.

If Sloane wanted to talk, she'd reach out. If she wanted Chicago more than him, he'd learn to live with it. Even if it destroyed him.

SLOANE LAY in bed at Bea's cottage, staring at the ceiling. Her phone was on the nightstand. Wesley's contact information pulled up. She'd typed and deleted a dozen messages.

I got the job offer.

I miss you.

I don't know what to do.

Please tell me what to do.

But she didn't send any of them. If Wesley wanted to talk,

he'd reach out. If he wanted her to stay, he'd say so. If she was worth fighting for, he'd fight.

Except.

What if Bea was right? What if she was expecting Wesley to fight without giving him any reason to think she wanted him to? What if they were both just scared? Sloane picked up her phone, started typing: *We should talk.*

But before she could send it, an email notification popped up. Morrison & Associates. Subject line: Formal Offer - URGENT.

Her heart pounded as she opened it. The offer was everything they'd promised. Six figures. Partnership track. Relocation assistance. Benefits package.

Start date: One week from today.

Due to client needs, we require your acceptance by Wednesday 5 PM EST. Please confirm.

Two days.

Great. She should have known getting the offer so early meant the deadlines would change. She had two days to decide between everything she'd worked for and everything she'd accidentally found.

CHAPTER 11

The wellness fair was tomorrow, and Sloane was throwing herself into organization like her life depended on it.

Because if she was busy checking vendor placements and coordinating electrical hookups, she didn't have to think about Wesley. Didn't have to remember the way he'd walked away from her three days ago. Didn't have to feel the constant ache in her chest every time she caught a glimpse of him across the fairgrounds.

"Move the yoga demo three feet to the left," she snapped at a volunteer. "No, your other left. There. Perfect."

Margot appeared at her elbow, yoga mat under her arm. "You and Wesley okay? The energy between you two is... tense."

"We're fine." The lie came easily. "Just stressed about the fair."

"Uh-huh." Margot's look was knowing. "That's why you've checked his vendor setup fourteen times and he keeps looking for you when he thinks no one's watching."

Sloane's chest constricted. "I need to check on the electrical panels."

She fled before Margot could push further.

Wesley smiled at Mrs. Jones as he demonstrated proper stretching techniques, but the smile didn't reach his eyes.

"You seem sad, Wesley," she observed. "Everything alright?"

"Just tired from fair prep," he lied.

"Hmm. Tired. Is that what we're calling heartbreak these days?"

Wesley's smile faltered. "I'm fine."

"You're a terrible liar, dear boy." She patted his hand. "But I won't pry. Just know that whatever you're running from usually catches up eventually."

After his demo ended, Wesley scanned the fairgrounds. His eyes found Sloane without conscious thought—she was arguing with a vendor about the payment app, looking fierce and competent and beautiful.

He missed her. Missed her laugh, her intelligence, the way she fit perfectly against him. Missed the sound of her voice, the sharpness of her wit, the surprising sweetness underneath all that grumpy armor.

Missed everything about her.

But she was leaving. Had gotten the job offer she'd been waiting for. Was going back to her real life, just like Devon had. Just like Wesley had known she would from the beginning.

So he stayed on his side of the fairgrounds and tried not to watch her.

He failed spectacularly.

. . .

AT 2 PM, the sky went dark.

Black clouds rolled over the mountains faster than seemed physically possible. Thunder rumbled in the distance. The wind picked up, sending vendor tents flapping and papers flying.

"Storm coming!" someone shouted.

Within minutes, chaos erupted. Vendors scrambling to secure merchandise. Volunteers running for cover. The elaborate setup they'd spent all day creating threatening to blow away.

Sloane's phone buzzed with emergency weather alerts. Severe thunderstorm warning. Possible tornado activity. Seek shelter immediately.

"Everyone inside!" Margot was shouting. "The community center! Now!"

But the elderly vendors were struggling with their equipment. The medical tent needed to be secured—supplies and medications exposed to potential wind damage. The sound system was still powered up, risking electrical fire if lightning hit.

Sloane went into crisis management mode.

"You three—help the vendors inside. You—secure the medical tent, medications first. You—kill power to the sound system." She was moving through the chaos, delegating, organizing, making split-second decisions.

This was what she was good at. Not just the organization, but helping people. Being part of a community that needed her.

And then she saw Wesley.

WESLEY WAS HELPING Mrs. Wicker secure her booth when he looked up and saw Sloane in full corporate commander mode. Directing volunteers, handling the crisis with competence and grace, completely in her element. This was the woman he'd fallen in love with—not despite her ambitious nature, but because of it.

"Thank goodness she's here," Mrs. Wicker observed. "Last time we were rained out, we lost most of the products. She's a natural leader."

"Yeah," Wesley agreed, his chest tight. "She is."

"You're a fool if you let her go, Wesley Nakamura."

"She already left."

"She's standing right there."

"For now." Wesley turned back to securing the booth. "But she's got a job offer in Chicago. Leaving next week."

"Did you ask her to stay?"

The question stopped him. "No."

"Why not?"

"Because I'm not going to make her choose between me an her dreams. I won't be that person who holds her back."

Mrs. Wicker made a disgusted sound. "You're so busy protecting her from having to choose that you're making the choice for her. That's not noble. That's cowardly."

Before Wesley could respond, a gust of wind tore through the fairgrounds, and a vendor tent went flying.

"Look out!"

Wesley moved on instinct, pulling Mrs. Wicker out of the way. The tent crashed where she'd been standing seconds before.

"Wesley!" Sloane was running toward them. "Are you okay?"

Their eyes met. The concern on her face, the fear that he might be hurt—it was real. Whatever was broken between them, she still cared.

"We're fine," Wesley said. "But we need to get everyone inside. Now."

. . .

The crisis forced them to communicate.

"I'll get the rest of the vendors," Sloane said. "You handle the medical equipment?"

"On it." Wesley was already moving.

They worked in tandem, professional at first, then warming as the urgency brought back their old rhythm. Small touches—his hand steadying her elbow, her fingers brushing his when they reached for the same supply crate. Shared looks across the fairgrounds as they coordinated the evacuation.

This was what they could be. If they trusted each other. If they were brave enough.

Within twenty minutes, everyone was inside the community center, safe and dry as the storm raged outside. The fairgrounds were a mess, but no one was hurt. And they might lose a tent or two, but essential oils, soaps and other wellness products were piled all around the walls.

Sloane stood in the doorway, watching the rain hammer down. Wesley came to stand beside her.

"Good work out there," he said quietly.

"You too." She didn't look at him. "That was close with Mrs. Wicker."

"Yeah."

Silence opened a chasm, loaded with everything they weren't saying.

"Sloane—"

Her phone rang.

Sloane looked at the screen. Chicago area code. Something's wrong.

"I need to take this."

She stepped outside onto the covered porch, watching the rain while her entire future hung in the balance.

"Hello, this is Sloane Hartwell."

"Ms. Hartwell, this is Jennifer from Morrison & Associates. We know we gave you until Monday, but we've had a development. Our client needs someone to start immediately. We need your answer now."

Sloane's heart pounded. "Now?"

"I'm sorry for the pressure, but it's either a yes immediately or we move to our second choice. The client won't wait."

Through the window, Sloane could see Wesley helping Mrs. Wicker with her coat. Could see the community she'd become a part of. Could see the life she'd accidentally built in six weeks.

Everything she thought she wanted versus everything she'd found.

"Can I have fifteen minutes?"

"Ten. That's all I can give you."

The line went dead.

Sloane stood in the rain, phone clutched in her hand, tears mixing with the storm.

WESLEY SAW her on the phone. Saw her face—shock, then panic, then something that looked like grief.

He knew immediately what it meant. The job offer. They wanted an answer. Probably now, given what he knew about how corporate firms operated.

Something broke in him. She was leaving. Of course she was leaving. He'd known this was coming since the day they met. But knowing and experiencing were different things.

He turned away so she wouldn't see his face. Couldn't watch her choose Chicago over him. Over this. Over them.

Mrs. Wicker touched his arm. "Go to her."

"She's made her choice."

"She hasn't made anything yet. But she will if you don't fight for her."

"I can't fight for someone who doesn't want to stay."

"How do you know she doesn't want to stay if you never asked?"

SLOANE WALKED BACK INSIDE, her clothes damp from the rain.

Wesley was across the room, deliberately not looking at her.

This was it. The moment she'd been working toward for months. The career, the prestige, the validation that she was still worth something after being laid off. Everything she thought she wanted.

So why did it feel like she was about to lose everything that mattered?

She pulled Wesley aside, into a quiet corner. "That was Morrison & Associates. They need an answer now. The client won't wait."

Wesley's face went carefully blank. "Congratulations."

"Wesley—"

"You should take it." His voice was steady, controlled. "It's what you've been working toward."

"Is that all you have to say?"

"What do you want me to say?" His control cracked slightly. "That I'll wait for you to come back on weekends? That we'll make long-distance work? We both know how this ends."

"Do we?"

"Yes." Wesley's voice turned cold, self-protective. "I won't be someone's safety net. Won't be the guy you come back to when Chicago gets exhausting."

Each word felt like a knife. "That's not fair—"

"You deserve that career, Sloane." His eyes were dark with

pain. "You deserve everything you've worked for. But I deserve someone who chooses me. Who chooses this life."

"You're not even giving me a chance to choose—"

"Because I can't!" Wesley's composure shattered. "I can't be the reason you give up your dreams and then resent me for it in five years. I can't watch you sacrifice everything you've worked for and wonder if you'll wake up one day regretting it."

"So you're making the choice for me?"

"I'm protecting both of us." His voice broke. "Go, Sloane. Take the job. Build the life you're supposed to have."

He turned and walked away before she could respond.

Sloane stood frozen, watching him leave. She wanted to run after him. To tell him he was wrong, that she'd choose him, that the job didn't matter.

But it did matter. Didn't it? She'd spent eight years building toward exactly this opportunity. Turning it down would be admitting defeat. Admitting that her entire career plan had been wrong.

Except.

If this was such a victory, why did it feel like she'd lost everything that mattered?

The storm passed. The fairgrounds were a mess but salvageable. Vendors began the cleanup, volunteers working together to restore order.

Sloane and Wesley stayed on opposite sides of the space, carefully avoiding each other.

At 4:30 PM, Sloane's phone rang again. Jennifer.

"Ms. Hartwell, we need your answer."

Sloane looked across the fairgrounds at Wesley. He was helping an elderly man secure a fallen tent, laughing at something the man said. Being exactly who he was—kind, patient, genuinely good.

Everything she'd been running from her entire life.

Everything she was terrified to want.

"Ms. Hartwell?"

Sloane closed her eyes. "I—"

THAT EVENING, Sloane came home in a daze. She'd given her answer to Morrison & Associates. Had made her choice.

Now she just had to live with it.

Bea was on the porch, waiting with a large glass of wine. The bottle was beside her on a small table, and an empty glass for Sloane.

"How was the fair?"

"Disaster. The storm shut us down. Wesley and I aren't speaking. And I got an ultimatum from my new boss."

"Ah." Bea poured tea calmly. "And what did you decide?"

Sloane sank into a chair, staring at nothing. "I don't know if I decided right."

"Tell me what happened."

"They needed an answer immediately. Wesley told me to take it. Said he wouldn't be my safety net, that I deserved the career and he deserved someone who chose him." Sloane's voice cracked. "He walked away before I could tell him—"

"Tell him what?"

"That I wanted to choose him. That I wanted to stay. But he didn't give me the chance."

Bea was quiet for a long moment. "What do you want, darling? Not what you think you should want. Not what makes sense on paper. What do you actually want?"

Sloane looked at her phone. GPS directions to Chicago already loaded.

Then she looked at Millbrook Falls—the mountains, the

waterfall, the town that had become home without her noticing.

"I want Wesley," she whispered. "I want this life. I want to wake up excited about my day instead of anxious. I want to measure success by happiness instead of salary. I want—"

"Then why are you sitting here?"

"Because he walked away. Because he made it clear he doesn't want me if I'm not sure. Because I'm terrified that if I choose him and it doesn't work out, I'll have given up everything for nothing. And what would I do here? I need to make money."

"And if you choose Chicago and wonder for the rest of your life what might have been?"

Sloane didn't have an answer.

She sat on Bea's porch until the stars came out, phone in her hand.

The job started Monday. She had to leave Sunday.

Tomorrow.

CHAPTER 12

Sunday morning, Sloane packed her car while Bea watched from the porch.

She'd said yes to Morrison & Associates. Had given her notice to Bea's care coordinator. Had mapped the route to Chicago and her new corporate apartment.

Everything was going according to plan.

So why did it feel like this was the biggest mistake of her life? how could she be so different in such a short time?

"I'm doing the right thing," Sloane said, more to herself than to Bea. "Aren't I?"

"The right thing for whom?"

Sloane stopped, a box of clothes suspended halfway into the trunk. "What do you mean?"

"I mean—is this right for you? Or is it right for the person you think you're supposed to be?"

"I'm supposed to want this. I worked so hard to get back to corporate consulting."

"Supposed to." Bea's smile was sad. "Those are interesting words, darling. Not 'I want this.' Not 'I'm excited for this.' Supposed to."

Sloane closed the trunk with more force than necessary. "I have to go. I start tomorrow."

"You could call them. Explain you've changed your mind."

"I can't just—" Sloane stopped. "Wesley told me to take the job. He made it very clear he didn't want me if I wasn't sure."

"Did he? Or did he push you away because he was scared?"

Sloane didn't have an answer for that.

She hugged Bea goodbye, promised to visit, drove away from Millbrook Falls with tears already streaming down her face.

Halfway to Chicago, she pulled over on the side of the highway and sobbed.

"WESLEY, DARLING, YOU LOOK TERRIBLE."

Mrs. Patterson settled into his treatment chair with a concerned expression. It was Wednesday, three days since Sloane had left, and Wesley was going through the motions of his life like a robot.

"I'm fine," he lied.

"You're a terrible liar. Everyone in town is asking about Sloane. Where is she? When is she coming back?"

Wesley focused on adjusting the resistance bands. "She went back to her life. Chicago. New job. It's what she wanted."

"Is it? Because Bea Kinsley says that girl cried for two hours before leaving."

Wesley's hands stilled. "She what?"

"Cried. Sobbed. Didn't want to go. Bea tried to convince her to stay, but Sloane kept saying she 'had to' take the job." Mrs. Patterson's gaze was sharp. "Almost like someone told her she should."

The words landed like a punch.

After his session with Mrs. Patterson, Wesley found Cora waiting in the clinic lobby with coffee and a determined expression.

"We need to talk."

"I'm busy—"

"You're wallowing. There's a difference." Cora pushed him into his office and closed the door. "Are you going to fight for her or just let her go?"

"What am I supposed to do? She made her choice."

"Did she?" Cora's voice was sharp. "Or did you push her away before she could choose you?"

"I was protecting—"

"Yourself. You were protecting yourself." Cora sat on the edge of his desk. "Wesley, I love you, but you're being an idiot. You fell for someone who scared you because she might leave, and instead of fighting for her, you made sure she left. That's not noble. That's self-sabotage."

Wesley sank into his chair, running his hands through his hair. "I'm scared, Cora. Every person I've cared about leaves. My parents moved to Seattle. Devon left. Sloane's leaving. Maybe I'm the problem."

"Or maybe you keep pushing people away before they can prove they'll stay." Cora's voice softened. "Sloane isn't Devon. She didn't leave for ambition. I'm betting she left because you told her to."

The truth he hadn't wanted to face crashed over him.

He'd pushed Sloane away. Had told her to take the job, build her life, go be successful somewhere else. Had protected his heart by breaking hers.

"What do I do?"

Cora grinned. "You go get her, you idiot. You show up and you fight."

. . .

THE MORRISON & Associates office occupied the fortieth floor of a glass tower in downtown Chicago. Corner offices, important clients, corporate prestige—everything Sloane had been working toward.

Her first day had been orientation. Her second day had been client meetings. Now, on her third day, she sat at her pristine desk staring at spreadsheets and feeling absolutely nothing.

The office felt sterile. The people felt interchangeable. Nobody asked how Bea was recovering or cared that she'd learned to kayak or wanted to hear about the wellness fair disaster.

At lunch, Sloane sat alone in the cafeteria and watched a couple at the next table laugh together. They had the ease of partners who chose each other every day, who knew each other's coffee orders and inside jokes and how to make each other smile.

She'd had that with Wesley. For six weeks.

And she'd thrown it away for this.

Her phone buzzed. Email from her new boss with fourteen attachments and the subject line: URGENT - Client deliverable by EOD.

Sloane stared at it, feeling nothing. She was measuring the wrong things again. This career didn't make her happy. It made her accomplished. There was a difference.

A huge, terrifying, life-changing difference.

BEA CALLED Wesley after he closed the clinic.

"Wesley, darling, we need to talk."

"If this is about Sloane—"

"Of course it's about Sloane. That girl is miserable in Chicago. Absolutely miserable." Bea's voice was firm. "And you're miserable here. This is ridiculous."

"She chose—"

"Because you told her to! Wesley Nakamura, I have never known you to be a coward, but you're being one now."

The words stung. "What am I supposed to do?"

"Go get her. Tell her how you feel. Fight for what you want."

"What if she says no? What if the job is more important?"

Bea's voice gentled. "Then at least you'll know you tried. But Wesley, darling—that girl loves you. She's just terrified of admitting it."

After hanging up, Wesley sat in his dark apartment, thinking. He'd been so busy protecting his heart he'd forgotten to fight for what he wanted.

Devon had left, yes. But Devon had never loved Millbrook Falls. Had never looked at Wesley like he hung the moon. Had never challenged him and respected him and made him laugh until his sides hurt.

Sloane was different.

And he'd let her go without a fight. And why did he need everyone else to tell him what to do?

Wesley grabbed his keys.

THE FLIGHT to Chicago took four hours with all the waiting. Wesley spent the entire time rehearsing what he'd say, then discarding it, then starting over.

By the time he parked the rental car outside the Morrison & Associates building, his hands were shaking.

He could do this. He could walk into her fancy corporate office and tell her he loved her and beg her to come home.

Or he could turn around and go back to Vermont and spend the rest of his life wondering what might have been.

Wesley got out of the car.

. . .

SLOANE'S ASSISTANT knocked on her door. "There's someone here to see you in the lobby."

"Is it a client?" she checked her calendar, no appointments until tomorrow. "Why the lobby?"

"The concierge didn't say. It's a man and he asked for you specifically."

She took the elevator down, expecting a suit. The Henderson contract she's taken over was running a bit behind. Maybe the contact was here to push?

She stepped out at the ground floor and found Wesley in jeans and flannel, looking completely out of place among the marble and glass and corporate perfection.

Her heart stopped. "Wesley? What are you doing here?"

He turned at the sound of her voice, and the look on his face—vulnerable and determined and terrified—made her chest ache. "I came to fight for you."

"What?"

Wesley crossed the lobby until they were standing face to face. "I let you leave. Stood there like a coward and watched you drive away because I was scared. Scared you'd choose your career over me, scared I wasn't enough, scared of being hurt again."

"Wesley—"

"Let me finish." His voice shook slightly. "I'm more scared of not trying. More scared of letting you think I don't care enough to fight. So I'm here. In your fancy corporate lobby. Looking ridiculous. Ready to fight for what I want."

Sloane's eyes filled with tears. "I don't understand—"

"You were right to take this job." Wesley's voice cracked. "You worked hard for it, you earned it, and you deserve to feel proud. But Sloane—you also deserve to be happy. And I don't think this place makes you happy."

The truth of it hit her like a physical blow.

"I think you're measuring the wrong things again," Wesley continued. "Chasing achievement because you're scared that without it, you're not enough. But you've always been enough. You're brilliant and capable and the most competent person I've ever met. You don't need this job to prove your worth."

Tears flowed down her cheeks.

"So I'm here to ask—" Wesley took her hands, holding them between his own. "—what do you actually want? Not what you're supposed to want. Not what looks good on paper. What makes you happy? If it's this, I'll accept it."

"YOU," Sloane whispered. "You make me happy."

Admitting it felt like breaking and healing simultaneously.

"I took this job because I thought I had to prove I could get back what I lost. But Wesley, I don't want this." The words came faster now, desperate to get out. "I hate this office, I hate these people who don't care about anything but billable hours, I hate waking up without you."

Wesley's grip on her hands tightened.

"I love you," Sloane said, the words finally freed. "I think I've loved you since you challenged me to observe your methods and see the value in connection over efficiency. Since you made terrible puns and counted my smiles and looked at me like I was perfect even when I was being impossibly grumpy. I've just been too scared to admit that choosing you, choosing Millbrook Falls, choosing contentment—that none of that makes me a failure."

"You love me?" Wesley's voice was so quiet, Sloane almost missed the question.

"So much it terrifies me."

Wesley crossed the remaining distance and pulled her into his arms. "Say it again."

"I love you."

"Again."

"I love you, Wesley Nakamura. Even though you make terrible puns and hum while you work and are pathologically optimistic about everything."

He kissed her.

Right there in the Morrison & Associates lobby, in front of her new coworkers and the security guards and anyone else who happened to be watching. Kissed her like he'd been dying without her for three days. Like she was oxygen, and he'd been drowning.

When they separated, both breathing hard, Wesley rested his forehead against hers.

"Come home with me."

Sloane laughed through her tears. "I haven't even finished my first week."

"So quit. Or don't. Take a leave of absence. Figure out what you actually want to do."

"Quitting is my only option." Possibility opened up before her as she said the words—vast and terrifying and perfect. "I could freelance. Consult remotely. Help small businesses like I've been helping with the fair. Build something that's mine."

"You could do anything." Wesley's smile was sunshine incarnate. "As long as you do it in Millbrook Falls. With me."

Sloane kissed him again. "Take me home."

TWENTY MINUTES LATER, Sloane walked into her boss's office and quit.

"I appreciate the opportunity, but this position isn't the right fit for me."

Her boss sputtered. "You've been here three days—"

"Which is why I know it's not right. I'm sorry for the inconvenience, but my decision is final."

She cleaned out her desk—which barely took five minutes since she'd never unpacked—and walked out of Morrison & Associates with Wesley's hand in hers.

In the parking garage, she looked at her BMW. "I should probably sell this. It's ridiculous for Vermont roads."

Wesley laughed. "Don't you dare. I love watching you park that thing in front of the hardware store while Hank judges you. Plus the long drive back will be much nicer in the BMW than in a rental."

"I'm never going to fit in, am I?"

"You already fit in. You just didn't notice." Wesley pulled her close. "Everyone in Millbrook Falls loves you. They've been asking about you constantly. Mrs. Patterson threatened to drive to Chicago herself to bring you back."

"Really?"

"Really. You're one of us now. Whether you like it or not."

Sloane buried her face in his chest. "I like it. I really, really like it."

WESLEY CALLED AHEAD to warn Bea they were coming.

Apparently, Bea called the entire town.

When they pulled into Millbrook Falls at sunset, half the town was waiting in the square with a "WELCOME HOME SLOANE" banner.

"Oh my god," Sloane said, getting out of her car. "This is mortifying."

"This is small-town Vermont." Wesley took her hand. "Get used to it."

Cordelia was there with champagne. Mrs. Tennant had

brought homemade dumplings. Even Hank was there, gruffly admitting that the fair ran smoother with her organizing.

Margot hugged Sloane. "We knew you'd come back. Cora owes me twenty dollars."

"There was a betting pool on me?"

"Of course there was. This is Millbrook Falls." Margot grinned. "We have limited entertainment options."

Bea was waiting on a bench, her walking boot sticking out and her cane beside her. Sloane hoped she's gotten a ride. "Welcome home, darling."

Sloane ran to hug her aunt. "I'm so sorry—"

"Hush. You're here now. That's all that matters."

The celebration lasted hours. Food and drinks and laughter and the whole town welcoming her back like she'd been gone for years instead of four days.

WESLEY UNLOCKED HIS APARTMENT DOOR, and Sloane stepped inside.

It felt different from the last time she'd been here. Less like visiting, more like coming home.

"So," Wesley said, closing the door behind them. "You love me. I don't hear that enough."

"I do." Sloane turned to face him. "Is that okay?"

"It's perfect." Wesley crossed the room, backing her against the wall. "I've wanted you since I first charmed you with my excellent sense of humor."

"I was never charmed by your puns."

"Liar." He kissed her neck. "You smiled."

"That was a grimace of pain."

"It was smile number seven. I was keeping count."

Sloane's breath caught as his mouth found that sensitive spot below her ear. "You're impossible."

"You're grumpy." His hands slid beneath her shirt. Her skin warmed at his touch. "It's perfect."

"Wesley—"

"Yeah?"

"Less talking. More kissing."

"Yes ma'am."

He kissed her properly then, deep and thorough, backing her toward the bedroom. They left a trail of clothes—his flannel, her blouse, his shoes, her ridiculous heels that had never been meant for Vermont.

By the time they reached his bed, Sloane was breathless and wanting and completely, utterly sure.

"I love you," she whispered against his mouth.

"I love you too." Wesley pulled her down with him. "So much."

The rest was heat and hands and the perfect certainty of choosing each other.

Fall in Millbrook Falls was gorgeous.

Sloane stood at the window of her new office—a bright space above Wesley's clinic—and watched leaves drift past in shades of gold and crimson. Her laptop was open to a client proposal, her second mug of coffee cooling on the desk, and she was genuinely, contentedly happy.

She'd started her own consulting business. Remote work for small businesses, organizational systems for local companies, even some work with Vermont's tourism board. Nothing corporate, nothing soul-crushing. Just work that felt meaningful.

Some days she still got job alerts from firms. She deleted them without reading. That life felt like it belonged to someone else.

"Ready for lunch?" Wesley appeared in her doorway, still in his scrubs, hair adorably mussed.

Sloane saved her work and crossed to him. "Always."

He pulled her into a kiss, and she melted against him. Three months together, and it still felt new every time.

"How's the Watkins proposal coming?" Wesley asked.

"Good. I think they're going to accept." Sloane straightened his collar. "How's your morning?"

"Mrs. Patterson asked when we're getting married. Again."

Sloane laughed. "What did you tell her?"

"That she's very nosy and should mind her own business."

"Which she took well, I'm sure."

"She threatened to plan the wedding herself if we didn't hurry up." Wesley grinned. "So that's something to look forward to."

They walked to the diner hand in hand, stopping to chat with Mrs. Wicker about her tomatoes and Hank about fair plans for next year. This was her life now—small-town rhythms, community connections, measuring success by happiness instead of salary.

She'd never been better.

WESLEY WATCHED Sloane laugh at something Margot said, and his chest felt too full.

Sometimes he still couldn't believe his luck. That Sloane Hartwell, with all her credentials and ambition, had decided a small-town physical therapist was enough.

Not just enough. Everything.

The ring was hidden in his desk drawer. He'd bought it two weeks ago, had a proposal planned for Christmas at the overlook where they'd first really talked.

But for now, he was just enjoying their present. Morning

coffee together, kisses between appointments, dinners at his place that often turned into something more, weekends exploring Vermont together.

"You're staring," Sloane said, sliding into the booth beside him.

"I'm admiring."

"It's creepy."

"It's romantic."

"It's both." But she was smiling, leaning into him.

The waitress appeared with their usual orders without being asked. "You two are disgustingly cute. It's making the other customers nauseous."

"Good," Wesley said, kissing Sloane's temple. "That's our brand now."

After lunch, they walked back to the clinic through autumn sunshine. Sloane's hand in his, their steps synchronized, both heading home.

Across the street, Bea and Cordelia watched from the bookstore window.

"Well done, Beatrice." Cordelia sipped her tea. "Another successful match."

"We do good work, don't we?" Bea smiled with satisfaction.

"The best work." Cordelia's gaze shifted to someone walking past the window. "Speaking of which, have you met the librarian? Delia Mackenzie. Lovely girl. Very bookish. Brilliant but a bit lonely I think."

"Oh?" Bea's eyes gleamed. "How interesting."

"And there's a rare book dealer visiting next month. Runs an antiquarian bookshop in New York."

"Is that so?" Bea set down her tea. "Well, I'll be mobile by then. Shall we?"

"I thought you'd never ask."

Outside, Sloane and Wesley paused to kiss on the sidewalk, completely oblivious to the plotting happening around them. The maple trees glowed gold in the afternoon light, the waterfall rushed through downtown, and Millbrook Falls embraced them in all its small-town glory.

Happy endings weren't always the end.

Sometimes they were just the beginning.

WANT MORE

Ready for more Millbrook Falls?

When small-town librarian Delia Mackenzie impulsively pretends to be rare book dealer Thaddeus Smythe-Jones's girlfriend to rescue him from a gold-digging socialite, she never expects their fake relationship to feel so real—or that falling for a man from old-money Boston might cost her everything she values about herself.

Use the QR code below to get your copy of The Harvest Festival Fake.

FREE BOOK

Use the QR code below to claim your copy of The Matchmaking Pact and find out where the old ladies of Millbrook Falls got their passion for creating couples.

REVIEW

* * *

If you enjoyed reading The Summer Fair Trap please consider helping other readers to find the story by using the QR code to leave a review.

ALSO BY LUCY

For more books by Lucy
go to Go to her home page

ABOUT LUCY HENRY

Lucy Henry writes feel-good romcoms packed with chemistry, chaos, and charm. She lives for meet-cute mishaps, awkward moments that turn unexpectedly romantic, and characters who fall in love while tripping over their own feet. When she's not plotting her next fiasco-turned-fairytale, she's drinking too much coffee, binge-watching baking shows, and laughing at her own jokes—because someone has to.

ACKNOWLEDGMENTS

Writing might look like a solo act, but trust me—I'm not doing this without a whole cast of behind-the-scenes heroes. I've been lucky to have support, encouragement, and inspiration from so many corners that it's impossible to thank everyone properly—but I'm absolutely going to try.

My writing groups keep me creative and caffeinated: The Vancouver Writers Social Group pushes me to look at stories from fresh angles, The Royal City Literary Arts Society gives me the chance to learn from generous, talented writers, and The Other 11 Months group reminds me that finishing the words is half the battle. My critique partners—with their sharp eyes, spot-on instincts, and gentle "um, maybe not that?" comments—help shape every book into something I'm proud of.

And to my beta readers: thank you for catching the wobbly bits, cheering for the swoony ones, and reminding me that these stories may come from me, but they're made for you.

www.ingramcontent.com/pod-product-compliance
Lightning Source LLC
LaVergne TN
LVHW051001080826
845145LV00009B/2398

* 9 7 8 1 9 9 7 9 4 9 0 7 7 *